"Mr. Shawnessy, Would You Please Remove Yourself From This Room?" Cara Asked Tightly.

Killian leaned close, and she felt his warm breath fan over her cheek. "Call me sweetheart, and I'll leave."

He was playing a game with her, Cara knew that. And as much as she wanted to kill him for it, she also found it exciting, like nothing she'd ever experienced before. She stood naked, with only a towel separating her from this stranger, a man she'd never laid eyes on until a few hours ago. Her heart pounded furiously; she could barely catch her breath.

"Sweetheart," she whispered, still refusing to break contact with his eyes.

Immediately she wanted to snatch the single word back. The amusement she'd seen in his eyes only moments ago darkened to something else entirely. Something dangerous. Something primitive.

Dear Reader,

Welcome to Silhouette Desire—where you're guaranteed powerful, passionate and provocative love stories that feature rugged heroes and spirited heroines who experience the full emotional intensity of falling in love!

Wonderful and ever-popular Annette Broadrick brings us September's MAN OF THE MONTH with *Lean, Mean & Lonesome*. Watch as a tough loner returns home to face the woman he walked away from but never forgot.

Our exciting continuity series TEXAS CATTLEMAN'S CLUB continues with *Cinderella's Tycoon* by Caroline Cross. Charismatic CEO Sterling Churchill marries a shy librarian pregnant with his sperm-bank baby—and finds love.

Proposition: Marriage is what rising star Eileen Wilks offers when the girl-next-door comes alive in the arms of an alpha hero. Beloved romance author Fayrene Preston makes her Desire debut with *The Barons of Texas: Tess,* featuring a beautiful heiress who falls in love with a sexy stranger. The popular theme BACHELORS & BABIES returns to Desire with Metsy Hingle's *Dad in Demand*. And Barbara McCauley's miniseries SECRETS! continues with the dramatic story of a mysterious millionaire in *Killian's Passion*.

So make a commitment to sensual love—treat yourself to all six September love stories from Silhouette Desire!

Enjoy!

Joan Marlow Golan
Senior Editor, Silhouette Desire

Please address questions and book requests to:
Silhouette Reader Service
U.S.: 3010 Walden Ave., P.O. Box 1325, Buffalo, NY 14269
Canadian: P.O. Box 609, Fort Erie, Ont. L2A 5X3

KILLIAN'S PASSION
BARBARA McCAULEY

SILHOUETTE *Desire*®

Published by Silhouette Books

America's Publisher of Contemporary Romance

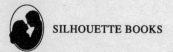 SILHOUETTE BOOKS

ISBN 0-373-76242-9

KILLIAN'S PASSION

Visit us at www.romance.net

Printed in U.S.A.

Books by Barbara McCauley

Silhouette Desire

Woman Tamer #621
Man from Cougar Pass #698
Her Kind of Man #771
Whitehorn's Woman #803
A Man Like Cade #832
Nightfire #875
Texas Heat #917
Texas Temptation #948
Texas Pride #971
Midnight Bride #1028
The Nanny and the Reluctant Rancher #1066
Courtship in Granite Ridge #1128
Seduction of the Reluctant Bride #1144
†*Blackhawk's Sweet Revenge* #1230
†*Secret Baby Santos* #1236
†*Killian's Passion* #1242

*Hearts of Stone
†Secrets!

BARBARA McCAULEY

was born and raised in California and has spent a good portion of her life exploring the mountains, beaches and deserts so abundant there. The youngest of five children, she grew up in a small house, and her only chance for a moment alone was to sneak into the backyard with a book and quietly hide away.

With two children of her own now and a busy household, she still finds herself slipping away to enjoy a good novel. A daydreamer and incurable romantic, she says writing has fulfilled her most incredible dream of all— breathing life into the people in her mind and making them real. She has one loud and demanding Amazon parrot named Fred and a German shepherd named Max. When she can manage the time, she loves to sink her hands into fresh-turned soil and make things grow.

To my daughter, Teri, who always reminds me to keep
my priorities straight. I love you, sweetheart.

One

Damn woman.

Killian Shawnessy's patience ran out at exactly 5:52 p.m. He'd already given up the idea of fishing today. The lake had turned choppy, and storm clouds were swelling on the horizon. It was also so blasted hot and humid he thought he was in a steam bath instead of a Texas mountain cabin.

Leaning against the cabin porch rail, he tossed back the last of a cold beer, wiped at the sweat on his brow, then frowned darkly at a clump of tall cattails on the other side of the lake where the fool woman was hiding.

He had no idea who the Peeping Thomasina was, or why she'd been watching him with binoculars for the past three hours. It was possible that Jordan had sent someone; Ian wouldn't put it past the woman, even though she'd sworn not to bother him for two weeks if he took the Cairo assignment.

But a promise didn't mean a rat's behind to his boss, Ian

knew. In the first two days alone, she'd already called four times. Yesterday Ian had simply unplugged the phone.

Which might explain the woman watching him, he thought with a scowl.

He'd only caught a glimpse of her when he'd checked her out with his own binoculars from inside the house. Slender, blond, on the tall side, maybe around five foot eight or nine. Dressed in boots and khakis and definitely inexperienced in the art of surveillance.

She wouldn't last long out there. Between the heat and the humidity and the approaching storm, she'd be gone within the hour. If she wasn't, the mosquitoes would be coming out for supper and they'd simply carry her off.

He didn't much give a damn. He still had eleven blissful days that he didn't have to report or answer to anyone. He'd come back to his hometown of Wolf River to see Nick Santos get married, and that was what he intended to do.

That was *all* he intended to do, other than fish, consume beer and watch spiders build webs.

A slight movement in the cattails caught his attention. Maybe Jordan needed a message sent back to her, Ian thought with a frown. And maybe this woman was the one to carry it.

At the first low rumble of thunder, Cara Sinclair knew she was in trouble. It wasn't bad enough that it was so hot and humid her eyeballs were melting. Now it had to go and rain, too. And based on the size of the black clouds crowding the once-blue sky, and the smell of the storm in the air, it was going to be a whopper.

Great, just great. She lowered her binoculars and wiped at the sheet of moisture on her forehead, then blinked to clear her eyes. So much for the glamorous job of a private investigator.

Not that she was into glamour; she would hardly be lying in a thicket of cattails wearing camouflage overalls if elegance and high fashion were her style. Big diamonds and fancy clothes were for the uptown debutantes of Philadelphia society, not for a girl from a small town like Bloomfield County. She'd take a baseball game over the ballet anyday, Cara thought, lifting the binoculars once again.

Now where had Mr. Killian Shawnessy disappeared to?

Focusing the binoculars, she scanned the porch he'd been sitting on for most of the afternoon. He must have gone back into the cabin, probably for another beer, Cara decided. It was certainly hot enough, and though she'd never acquired the taste herself, on a day like today, anything cold and bubbly would be welcome. She stared at the lake, fantasized about jumping into the cool water, then sighed and concentrated on the job at hand.

At least if she had to lie in these rough, itchy weeds in this miserable gray heat and watch someone, she had a good subject. Killian Shawnessy definitely fit into the category of superhunk. Tall, thick black hair, strong square jaw. A face that was a combination of construction-worker-rugged and magazine-cover handsome. Those long legs of his filled out a pair of jeans like nobody's business; that broad chest and muscular arms under the chambray shirt he wore were enough to make a girl's heart skip a beat or two in appreciation. She couldn't tell what color his eyes were, but she'd bet her brand-new-not-even-paid-for-yet 500 mm zoom lens that they were brown. Dark brown.

Not that she intended to get close enough to find out. Not yet, anyway. For now she simply needed to take a few pictures and watch him for a couple of days, then report back to Margaret.

And based on how friendly and talkative the people of Wolf River were, she'd have plenty to report.

Tracy Simpson, a fence-post-thin brunette working the cash register at the Stop N Shop in town, had turned into a regular Chatty Cathy this morning when Cara casually mentioned the name Killian Shawnessy.

"You know Ian?" Surprise lifted Tracy's heavily lined eyebrows.

Cara shrugged and started to browse through a display of paperbacks beside the counter. "A friend of a friend. Said if I was passing through here to say hi."

"Must be your lucky day," Tracy said with amazement. "Ian's been gone nearly fourteen years, but showed up three days ago. Is that a coincidence or what?"

"Incredible." Cara could hardly tell the woman she'd followed Ian here from Washington, D.C. "Back to visit his folks?"

"Ian's got no folks, unless you count Esther Matthews. She was his foster ma for a spell, but she passed on a couple years back. Ian's here for Nick Santos and Maggie Smith's wedding next week."

"Nick Santos?" Cara glanced up from the mystery novel she'd been eyeing. "That wouldn't be *the* Nick Santos, would it, as in Three-Time National Champion Motorcycle Racer?"

"One and the same," Tracy chirped brightly. "Don't that beat all, a celebrity like Nick Santos living right here in Wolf River?"

It sure did, Cara thought, and added the mystery novel to the bottled water and chocolate bar she'd already set on the counter. She'd been a Nick Santos fan ever since her brother Gabe had taken her to her first race when she was seventeen. More than one woman's heart had been broken when Santos retired from racing.

Miniature silver cowboy boots dangled at Tracy's ears as she rang up the order. "Nick and Lucas Blackhawk were the closest thing to a family that Ian ever got, him being abandoned as a baby and all. Those three boys were tight as Old Lady Appleby's hair bun. Hey, you want some dried apricots? We got them on special today. Two packages for a dollar.''

"Sure, I'll take four." Anything to keep the woman talking. Especially about Ian. "You say Ian was abandoned?"

"Right on the church steps, was the story I heard growing up. But then, there were lots of stories about Ian Shawnessy, especially when he got old enough to buckle his own belt." Tracy gave a wicked wink. "If you know what I mean."

Cara had a pretty good idea, but she'd rather not go there. "So he's staying with Nick until the wedding?" she asked nonchalantly, sliding a box of cheese crackers across the counter.

"Shoot, no. He's got himself holed up in one of Harper Whitman's rental cabins up at Silver Tree Lake. He came in here three days ago and bought enough food to feed a small country, so I reckon he's staying a spell."

Using one long red nail, the brunette punched in the cracker price on the cash register. "Thought I might be neighborly and check up on him in a day or two, see if he has everything he needs up there. That'll be twelve-oh-five."

Cara's next trip to the real estate and recreational rental office across the street proved to be another warehouse of information, as well. Beverly Patterson, the apple-cheeked, gray-haired office manager, pleasantly informed Cara that there were indeed rentals still available by Silver Tree Lake.

"Are there other cabins rented?" Cara gave Beverly what she hoped was a timid look. "I don't mean to be nosy, it's just that being a woman up there alone and all, well, I thought I might feel safer knowing who else was around."

"A woman can't be too careful." Beverly nodded in understanding. "But don't you worry, dear. There's a couple on their honeymoon just checked into cabin six at the farthest end of the lake, and Ian Shawnessy's in cabin three. I'll put you in cabin four right next to him."

"Ian?" Cara's insides did a tap dance, but she kept her voice tiny and her expression worried. "Is he someone you know?"

"Land sakes," Beverly said with a flip of her hand, "everyone in Wolf River knows Ian. But don't you go listening to any stories about him. Just kicked up a little dust before he went off to join the Army, that's all, and that trouble twenty years ago with Hank Thompson was never deserved. Some folks just don't have the good sense to let go of an old bone. Ian Shawnessy is a fine boy. You have any problems up there, you just give him a holler."

Cara was about to ask what the trouble with Hank Thompson had been when the bell over the office door jangled. Two men dressed in fishing gear—one stocky, with silver hair, and one slender, younger, with a blond crew cut—came through the door.

"I'll be right with you gentlemen." Beverly smiled at the men, then turned back to Cara and slid a key across the counter. "All the cabins have phones, dear. If you need anything, just give a call."

She made a quick trip to the market, then found the road off the main highway that led to Silver Tree Lake. The two-lane road was narrow and wound upward through thick dogwood and pines. Twenty minutes later she'd unloaded her groceries and gear from her Jeep into her cabin, zipped on her overalls and grabbed her backpack.

Piece of cake, she'd thought when she'd settled herself into the tall weeds across the lake and found her man lazing on the front porch of his cabin. She snapped a roll of pictures, munched on dried apricots and crackers and replayed *Casablanca* in her mind to pass the time.

But as the heat settled in and the humidity rose steadily over the next three hours, that piece of cake began to quickly crumble.

When the first big drop of rain hit her on the cheek, the cake all but dissolved. The next drop splashed on her nose at the same time thunder rumbled the ground and lightning zigzagged across the dark sky. Cara might be the first one to admit she'd done a lot of foolish things, but never stupid. She at least knew enough to get out of a lightning storm. Tomorrow was always another day, as the saying went.

Tossing her binoculars into her backpack, she rose on her hands and knees and started to crawl backward out of the thick cattails.

And froze when she hit something very solid.

And very human.

Slowly she glanced over her shoulder, then swallowed hard at the sight of one Killian Shawnessy towering over her.

"Hi, there." He stared down at her; the tight smile on his mouth did not reach his narrowed eyes.

She opened her mouth to respond, but the only sound that came out was a whoosh of air when he lunged, then neatly flipped her onto her back and pinned her down. Even in this suddenly embarrassing and demeaning situation, Cara had to admit that he was good.

Damn good.

Nonetheless, he was also a man. And with him lying on top of her like he was, he was almost in perfect alignment for her best and most effective move, a move that would have him singing soprano for days.

Adrenaline pumped wildly through her blood, but despite her finely honed instinct to slam her knee upward, she clenched her teeth together and resisted. She didn't come here to hurt him, after all.

"You wanna tell me why you've been spying on me all afternoon?" he asked smoothly.

She forced her heartbeat to slow down and struggled to concentrate on his face rather than the press of his hard body against hers. His expression was calm, but his jaw was set tight, his eyes as sharp and focused as a cat with a mouse under its paw. What a strange time to notice that his eyes *were* brown, as she'd guessed. Deep, dark brown, with a black ring around the iris.

Eyes like Margaret Muldoon's.

"Who the hell do you think you are?" She feigned indignation and made a pitiful attempt to pull away from his grip. She'd always found it to her advantage to pretend weakness until her opponent was off guard and the time was right. "Get off me."

To her annoyance, his large hands tightened their hold on her wrists. He leaned closer, his broad chest pressing her down into the cattails. Sweat dripped down his throat and disappeared into the open collar of his shirt. The scent of hot skin and pure masculinity clung to him.

"I asked you a question, Blondie. I want an answer. Now."

Blast it, if the man wasn't solid muscle and outweighed her by at least seventy pounds. But what she lacked in strength she always made up for in endurance and timing, both of which were on her side at the moment. She didn't want to hurt him, but if he didn't let go of her soon, her pride would insist on taking over. Especially after the Blondie crack. Lord, how she hated those obnoxious little names men gave women.

What had been a heavy sprinkle of rain gradually increased, and Cara blinked the drops out of her eyes. "Look,

buster—'' she chose her own annoying little name for him
''—this isn't private property and I'm not trespassing. I'm
renting the next cabin down, and I was just taking in a little
scenery while I'm on vacation, not that it's any of your
business.''

''Is that so?'' He scanned the length of her. ''You always
take in the landscape on your stomach with binoculars?''

''I'm a bird watcher. Last I heard there's no law against
that.''

One shock of dark hair fell over his damp forehead as
he considered her answer. ''What bird?''

''What bird?'' *What bird...what bird...* Damn. She
knew nothing about birds.

Impatience deepened his frown. ''What bird have you
been watching for the past three hours?''

''Oh. A three-toed, yellow-rumped sapsucker. It's nest-
ing in that Douglas fir twenty yards off your cabin. Very
rare.'' She prayed there was a bird up there. *Any* bird, or
something that even remotely resembled a nest.

''Is that right?'' He lifted his gaze to the thick grove of
trees and stared. ''Three-toed sapsucker, huh?''

''Yellow-rumped,'' she hissed through clenched teeth.
''Now get off me.''

The weight of his body matched the heavy gaze he
dropped back down to her. The lines on his face were hard,
angular, like his body, and the intensity of his narrowed
gaze made her breath catch.

He shook his head slowly. ''We can do this the easy way
or the hard way, sweetheart. It's your choice.''

She didn't know what he meant by *this,* but she had no
intention of *doing* anything with this jerk. She let her body
go slack and turned her head away, as if she were acqui-
escing to him.

''All right.'' She dragged in a shuddering, pathetic

breath. "I guess we'll do it—" her knee came up hard and fast and right on target "—the *hard* way."

Ian sucked in his breath as the first blast of pain ripped through the lower half of his body. Stars exploded in front of his eyes as a wave of nausea washed over him. Her voice had sounded so weak and frightened that he'd let his guard down for one, sympathetic moment. A moment he was now paying for dearly.

"Now get off me!," he heard the woman yell through the sea of agony he was drowning in.

He'd collapsed on top of her, and she shoved furiously at his chest. Even if he'd wanted to, he hadn't the strength to move. He'd been annoyed before, but now he was downright *mad.* She was definitely going to pay for this, and so was Jordan. Big-time.

He gulped in a deep lungful of air, swore heatedly on the exhale. Her clawed fingers were plowing toward his face when he caught her wrists just in time. Using one hand, he pinned her hands over her head again. With his other hand he reached behind him and pulled out the rope he'd tucked into the waistband of his jeans before he'd left the cabin.

Her big green eyes widened at the sight of the rope, and for the first time he saw fear there. He'd been careful not to hurt her before, but that was before she set the rules between them, or rather, eliminated the rules. He wasn't taking any more chances with this one, and if she got roughed up, that was her choice.

She bucked under him like a crazed bronco.

"Did I ever tell you I spent six months working a cattle ranch?" He had her hands wrapped and tied in two seconds, then moved to her kicking feet. Two more seconds and they were bound, as well. "They called me Flash."

Her eyes spit green fire while she called him a few names

of her own. Lightning punctuated one especially rude exclamation she shot at him; thunder drowned out the next. If nothing else, Ian noted, she certainly was creative with her expletives.

With another loud crack of thunder, the sky opened up on them.

The cattails bowed under the driving force of the hot rain; the lake turned gray and frothy. Lifting his head, Ian cursed at the sky; the rain blasted him with the force of liquid bullets.

Dammit, dammit, dammit.

He swiped at his face and stared back at the hog-tied woman. He'd planned on leaving her out here to stew for a while, but in this weather, she'd end up shish-kebab if a lightning bolt zapped her. When the heel of her boot caught his knee he grunted sharply, considered dumping her into the lake, then swore again as he bent and flung her over his shoulder. She gave a loud *ommph,* and he was momentarily blessed with her silence while she gasped for breath.

Her wiggling body was slender but firm under her overalls, her legs long and powerful. Any other time, any other place, he would have appreciated those attributes in a woman. Her knee caught his chin and slammed his teeth together, reminding him this was definitely not any other time or place. He stilled her thrashing with a none-too-gentle grip around her knees.

"I believe a little gratitude is in order here, Blondie." He quickly scooped up her backpack before she could knee him again. "If I left you out here, you'd either be a crispy critter or drowned, probably both."

She expressed her gratitude with a fresh and imaginative onslaught of opinions of him and what she intended to do to him at the first opportunity. He winced at one especially descriptive suggestion and decided he had better make certain she never had the chance.

Lightning speared a tree fifty feet away, exploding a huge branch. The woman miraculously ceased struggling. The air crackled with electricity and the scent of burned pine.

"Would you quit lollygagging and get us inside?" she yelled over the storm and kicked him, only this time he knew it was to hurry him up. Annoyed, but just as eager as she was to get out of the storm, he ran back around the lake, bouncing her the entire way. It wasn't an easy ride, but it was a fast one.

They were both soaking wet by the time he kicked the cabin door shut behind him. He dumped the woman unceremoniously on the hardwood floor in front of the unlit rock fireplace and stood over her. With her ponytail plastered to her head and her drenched overalls, the term drowned rat came to mind. She sat in a spreading pool of water, fury darkening her moss-green eyes.

He glared at her. She glared right back.

"Untie me," she demanded.

"'Fraid not." He dragged his hands through his dripping wet hair, then scraped the rain off his face. "Not until I get some answers."

"Mrs. Patterson is going to hear about this," she sputtered at him through the water dripping down her face.

"Mrs. Patterson?" He lifted one brow. "As in Beverly Patterson at the real estate office?"

"That's right. When she rented me the cabin next to yours she said I'd be safe up here, and that you were a fine boy I could trust. She obviously doesn't know you like to tie women up for sport and kidnap them."

"For a woman who's been tied up and kidnapped," he

said dryly, "you've got quite a mouth on you. Maybe you like that sort of thing."

She swung her heavy boot out at him, and he yelped when she made contact with his shin. He jumped away as she drew back for a second blow. Narrowing his eyes to fierce slits, he rubbed at his leg and growled at her. "I had no intention of hurting you. At least, I didn't, but you certainly know how to change a man's mind."

When she lifted her chin and pointed it indignantly at him, Ian couldn't help but notice the delicate shape of her face; her cheekbones were high, her skin smooth, her lips wide and lush. Too bad that gorgeous mouth of hers didn't know when to quit.

"You don't scare me." She tossed back her head. "I have four brothers, every one of them mean as a rattlesnake and big as a Mack truck. They'll hunt you down, and when they're done with you, folks will be calling you Jigsaw instead of Flash."

In spite of himself, he almost laughed. He had to admire her spunk, especially considering which side of those ropes she was on. He wasn't sure if she was lying about the brothers, but he was damn certain she was fibbing about why she was up here in the mountains.

He picked up her backpack that he'd dropped on the floor beside her. "Well now, what have we here." He smiled at her. "Let's have a look, shall we?"

"That's my personal property, and if you know what's good for you, you'll stay out of it," she threatened, but he caught the edge of distress in her voice.

"Blondie, if I knew what was good for me, I'd have left you tied up in the cattails."

As if to punctuate his statement, thunder rattled the cabin's windows and rain pounded the roof. They'd brought the scent of the storm in with them, and the air inside the small cabin was as thick as it was hot.

Her jaw clamped tight as he snapped open the backpack. "Nice camera." He pulled out an expensive 35mm Nikon and gave a soft whistle of appreciation. "You could take pictures of moon craters with this baby."

"I'm a photographer for a nature magazine. I need a powerful lens."

"Then I'm sure all this film—" he ignored her gasp when he rewound the film, then popped open the camera case "—has pictures of yellow-rumped sapsuckers and furry little critters, right? There's a one-hour in town. How 'bout I take them in for you and develop them?"

"How 'bout you eat dirt and die?" she said sweetly.

Despite the foul mood she'd put him in, he grinned at her, then turned his attention back to her bag. He pulled out a small, brown leather wallet and flipped it open. "Let's see if you have a name other than Blondie. Ah, here it is. Sinclair." He held up her driver's license. "Cara Sinclair." He glanced up sharply. "Philadelphia?"

She said nothing, just shot poison arrows at him while water dripped off her pert little nose. Jordan didn't have any agents in Philadelphia that Ian knew of. And there would be no reason for his boss to pull an agent out of their own jurisdiction for a simple surveillance. He stared at the woman, wondered for one brief, horrible second if he might have made a mistake.

No. She was lying, all right. He might be wrong about her being an agent, but he wasn't wrong about the fact that she was lying through her perfectly straight, beautifully white teeth.

So why the hell had she been watching him, then?

Her driver's license appeared authentic; he could spot a fake from ten meters. It certainly described her accurately.

Five foot eight, blond. Green eyes, 125 pounds, though it was hard to tell under the heavy overalls she had on. She was twenty-six and lived in an apartment on Brooks Avenue in Philadelphia. Nothing ominous, nothing suspicious.

Ian ignored her continued protests while he flipped through the rest of her gear. Binoculars, bottled water, a package of dried apricots, three rolls of film. Nothing to link her to Jordan or any government agency, but nothing that confirmed her story about working for a nature magazine, either.

"If you're *through*," she said with enough ice in her voice to slice ten degrees off the heat in the room, "you can untie these ropes now."

If the southern section of his anatomy weren't still aching from contact with her knee, and his shin wasn't throbbing from that kiss from her boot, Ian would have appreciated the woman's nerve. Even tied up, soaking wet, she made demands with the air of an aristocrat.

Tossing the backpack onto the worn leather couch facing the fireplace, he hunkered down beside the woman, draping one arm casually over his knee while he studied his prey. Chin lifted, she stared right back, her eyes shooting green lightning bolts that matched the ferocity of the storm outside.

He leaned in close, brought his face within an inch of hers and caught the scent of raspberry drifting from her wet hair. "I'll make you a deal, Miss Sinclair. You tell me the truth, and maybe, just maybe, I'll let you go."

"I'll make *you* a deal, Shawnessy," she purred back. "You let me go, and maybe, just maybe, I'll let you live."

He chuckled, actually enjoying himself for the first time since this pain-in-the-butt had shown up. His laughter was cut short by the sudden pounding on his front door. The woman's eyes opened wide, then her mouth as she sucked in air to call out. He did the easiest and fastest thing he could do to shut her up.

He kissed her.

Two

Nothing could have possibly defused Cara more than the slam of Ian's mouth against hers. She'd drawn in a breath the same second his lips smothered hers, and her lungs held the air in stunned suspension. Her heart smashed against her ribs, once, twice, and still he didn't stop, only deepened the pressure with his strong, hard lips while he scooped her up in his arms.

She should bite him—pride and instinct both told her to—but she didn't. She couldn't. All she could do was...nothing. She had the most frustrating and infuriating urge to draw him closer still, but with her hands tied that was hardly possible.

There was no passion in his kiss, no sense of need or desire, but there was heat. A consuming, toe-curling, bone-melting fire that spread through her blood even as her mind screamed that she was an idiot. Nothing like this had ever happened to her before, and she had no defenses prepared for it, no protection.

He carried her somewhere, but she didn't even care where. His chest was solid and warm against her, his arms strong and muscular. They were both soaking wet, and it felt as if steam were rising from their skin and clothes. Clothes that suddenly felt tight and uncomfortable. His mouth stayed steady on hers, never letting up, and she felt as if she were drowning in the taste of him, something dark and heady and overwhelmingly masculine.

He made a sound deep in his throat, and she couldn't tell if it was annoyance or pleasure. He swung her sideways through a doorway, and for the briefest moment, so fleeting she wasn't certain if she imagined it, she felt his tongue sweep over her lips.

Her senses were still spinning when he dumped her unceremoniously into a bathtub. She heard a man's voice call Ian's name, and the sound snapped her out of her trance. She blinked twice and swung an elbow at his face, catching him in his bottom lip. His head snapped back and he swore, then grabbed a sock from a sports bag sitting beside the tub and shoved it into her mouth. A hand towel came next, and he secured it over her mouth with a knot at the base of her head.

Furious, she shook her head and screamed into the gag, praying the sock was clean while she plotted his demise. It was going to be slow and painful. Her only satisfaction at the moment was the blood oozing from his lip where she'd whacked him with her elbow. He wiped at his mouth with the back of his hand, scowled when he saw the blood, then rose and pointed a warning finger at her.

"I'm going to get rid of whoever that is. So help me, if you make one sound, I promise you that you'll be sorry."

She was already sorry, but she recognized that tone in

his voice. She'd heard it often enough in her brothers', when they'd been pushed to the edge of their tolerance. And since—for the moment—he obviously had the upper hand, she could be patient.

She still had a trick or two up her sleeve for Mr. Killian Shawnessy.

"You deaf or something?" Nick Santos, wearing a torn, sleeveless white T-shirt and faded jeans, strolled past Ian when he threw open the door. "I've been knocking out here for five minutes. How come your door's locked, anyway?"

"To keep bums like you out." Ian held his breath while he kept one eye on the bathroom door, half expecting a female fireball to explode through at any moment.

Nick shook his wet, dark hair and headed for the refrigerator. "Damn, it's hot. Got a cold one?"

Terrific, Ian thought on a curse. He could have easily gotten rid of anybody but Nick or Lucas. His day had swiftly moved from bad to worse, and the prospects of it improving were looking less than slim. Of course, he could always explain that he couldn't entertain company at the moment because he had a woman tied up in his bathtub. That ought to go over well.

Ian's hand tightened on the still-open front door. The rain had nearly stopped, but the heat hadn't let up. Humidity choked the air like a tight fist. "Look, Santos, this is kind of a bad time."

Nick gave a snort of laughter while he rummaged through the refrigerator, clanking bottles against cans. "You're in the middle of nowhere, with nothing to do, your best buddy drives twenty minutes in a downpour to come see you, and you tell him it's a bad time. You're a riot."

"I'm serious." Ian raked a hand through his still-wet hair. The woman had been quiet for all of sixty seconds.

A record. Strangely enough, the silence worried him. "I'm a little busy right now."

His quest successful, Nick pulled a cold bottle out of the refrigerator, then kicked the door shut while he twisted off the cap. "What, is it time for a poetry reading from the woodland nymphs?"

Amused with himself, Nick took a long swig from his bottle, then gave a loud sigh of appreciation. "Damn, that tastes good. Don't mind me, buddy. I'll just sit right here and drink my beer and you can go right ahead and do whatever it is you need to do. Oh, yeah, and I'm supposed to remind you about the tux fitting on Thursday morning and dinner Friday night at Lucas's house after the wedding rehearsal."

Muttering an oath under his breath, Ian shoved the door closed as Nick plopped down on the sofa. "Speaking of your wedding, don't you have to help Maggie pick out flowers or tablecloths or something?"

"I am helping. I'm staying out of the way." Nick tossed back another swallow of beer while he put his feet up on the weathered pine coffee table. "I've got three hours to kill before I pick my son up from his grandma's house."

Ian couldn't help but notice the pride in Nick's eyes at the mention of his son. A son he hadn't even known existed until a few weeks ago. Ian still couldn't believe it. Nick had a five-year-old son and was getting married in a few days to little redheaded Maggie Smith, who wasn't so little anymore. She was all grown-up and gorgeous.

And Lucas. Married to a blond beauty like Julianna Hadley, with twins. A boy and a girl. Damn if life didn't work in strange, mysterious ways.

Thank God at least *he* had kept his sanity, Ian thought with relief.

"Hey—" Nick gestured with the bottle in his hand "—did you know you're all wet?"

A noise from the bathroom, sort of a thump, had Nick turning his head.

The knot of tension in Ian's shoulders worked its way up his neck to his jaw. He had to get rid of Nick. Immediately.

"Squirrels," Ian said evenly. "They built a nest in the attic over the bathroom. I was on the roof trying to see where they got in when the storm hit. Listen, I've got to go into town and buy some screen to cover the vent up there. Meet me at Tanner's in forty-five minutes. I'll spring for the beer and pool."

Never mind that Nick could have bought the pool hall fifty times over, it was unthinkable to turn down a free game of pool and beer. "Make that ten bucks a game and you're on."

"Five. Take it or leave it." Ian knew if he gave in too easily, Nick might be suspicious.

"You're on." Not one to be wasteful, Nick took a deep swig from his bottle and started to rise. "I'll call Lucas, see if he can get away from Julianna and the kids for a couple of hours."

Another sound from the bathroom. A clank this time. Nick turned toward the bathroom. "Squirrels, you say?"

"They might be inside. I'll check it out." Ian started for the bathroom, but stopped at the distinct sound of water running from the sink faucet.

Nick swiveled a look at Ian. "They know how to turn on the water?"

The bathroom door opened, and she flounced out.

She'd stripped out of her wet khakis and was wearing a snug white tank top and tight jeans that exposed curves he hadn't seen before. She'd done something with her hair—

pulled it back and let a few wet strands curl around her freshly washed, heart-shaped face.

How the hell had she gotten out of that rope?

"Oh, Ian, honey, there you are." She smiled brightly at him, but it wasn't a smile that reached her smoky-green eyes—it was smug satisfaction. "I was wondering what took you so long. I'm afraid we'll have to do this some other time. I completely forgot I have an appointment in town. I'll call you later and—oh, you have company."

Nick's jaw had gone slack as he stared at the woman. If Ian wasn't so furious, he'd be laughing his butt off at the expression on his friend's face.

Hell, it had to be the same as the expression on his *own* face.

"I'll just get my bag and be on my way." She bent down to pick up her backpack and had started for the door when she stopped suddenly and turned to stare hard at Nick. Nick stared right back.

"Nick Santos?" Eyes wide, she whispered the name with reverence.

Nick managed an uncertain nod and continued to gawk openly at the woman.

"I've been a fan for years." She moved toward him, her smile genuine now as she offered her hand. "Cara Sinclair."

Nick stared at Cara's hand, blinked twice, then slowly closed his palm over her long, slender fingers. "Uh, a pleasure, Miss Sinclair."

"Cara, please," she said, her voice soft and breathy.

This *isn't* happening, Ian thought dimly. Five minutes ago he'd left this long-legged she-cat spitting and snarling in his bathtub. Tied up and gagged. Now she stood here as calmly as if she'd dropped in for tea, cooing that she was a *fan* of Nick's, for God's sake.

"I was at the Bloomfield County Speedway when you won Nationals three years ago." She pulled her hand away and shifted the backpack on her shoulder. "You were amazing."

Her eyes were soft now, almost dreamy, Ian noted, and he clenched his jaw so tightly he thought it might snap. If she asked Santos for his autograph, Ian knew he'd have to hurt someone.

"Just lucky, but thanks, anyway." Nick seemed to have his composure back now. He flashed Cara the smile that had graced numerous sports magazines and several advertising campaigns for everything from motorcycles to jeans to milk. Charm had always been Nick's middle name, and he laid it on heavy. Ian was certain it was just to annoy him.

Damn if it wasn't working.

"I'm off the circuit now," Nick said smoothly. "I've got my own place customizing bikes here in Wolf River. Maybe you'd like to see it sometime." Nick grinned at Ian, who scowled back. "Ian can bring you by."

Cara looked at Ian, and a slow smile spread over her lips, lips still slightly swollen and rosy from the kiss he'd planted on her. Or maybe it was from the sock he'd shoved in her mouth. Either way, the look she shot him said he'd better watch his back.

"Thanks. I'll get back to you on that. Oh, and congratulations on your upcoming wedding. Ian couldn't stop talking about it."

"Is that right?" Nick raised his brows and glanced at Ian. Ian knew what Nick thought, that he'd interrupted an afternoon interlude, not conversation about the Santos wedding. What else was he to think when a beautiful woman came bouncing out of the bathroom, her hair wet and her cheeks flushed?

And Ian decided he'd let Nick keep right on thinking just that.

Moving behind the Sinclair woman, Ian caught the scent of the storm that still lingered on her damp hair and smooth skin. When he placed his hands on her shoulders in what appeared to be an affectionate display, she stiffened, then covered his boot discreetly with her own and came down hard on his instep. Pain shot up his leg when she shifted her weight. She leaned intimately against him while she dug her heel in deeper. He forced a smile and plowed his fingers into the soft flesh of her shoulders.

"I'll catch you in town, Santos," Ian ground out, fighting to ignore the bone-crushing pressure of her boot on top of his foot. "I'd just like to say goodbye to Cara."

"I've really got to run, darling. I don't want to be late for my appointment." She twisted in his arms to press a kiss to his cheek and threw her entire weight into increasing his torture. He sucked in a breath and clenched his teeth.

She held his gaze, waited for him to make the next move. He considered his options: create a scene in front of Nick or let her go. He didn't like either option.

Neither he or the woman, for reasons of their own, wanted a confrontation in front of Nick. No, Ian thought as he slowly let go of her shoulders, he wanted to finish this privately, someplace where they would be completely alone.

There was a momentary, tense silence as she stepped away from him. The rain had stopped completely now and the only sound was the heavy *drip-drip* of water from the roof.

She turned away from him and smiled at Nick as she backed toward the door. "Nice to meet you."

Nick nodded. "You, too. We'll see you around."

Her hand on the open door, Cara paused and cast a

glance at Ian. "Maybe," she said, arching one delicate brow.

Ian stared at the door when she closed it behind her.

No maybe about it, Blondie.

She wouldn't go far, he was certain of that. She'd come here for something. Whatever it was she was after, she wasn't finished yet.

And neither was he.

He turned to Nick, who was staring hard at him. "Don't ask. Don't even ask."

Fortunately for Nick, he didn't. He simply scratched at his neck and shrugged. "Does this mean that free offer of pool and beer is on or off?"

"On." Ian unbuttoned his shirt and headed for the bedroom to change his clothes. He needed a game of pool to clear his head and a beer to wash the taste of apricots out of his mouth.

Cara kept a vigil on the thick trees separating her cabin from Ian's. Evening shadows darkened the woods, and though Cara had never been afraid of the night, she couldn't stop the prickle of anxiety working its way up her spine.

He hadn't followed her when she'd left his cabin over an hour ago, but she hadn't really expected that he would. At least, not yet. Through the bathroom door, she'd overheard Ian's offer to meet Nick in town for a game of pool, and she assumed that he'd stayed with those plans. No doubt Ian would play it cool, to downplay what Nick had walked into this afternoon.

Or what he *thought* he'd walked into.

She smiled at that, decided that Ian would stay in town, casually play a few games of pool, drink some beer. He'd act like he had all the time in the world. But Cara knew he was thinking about her, wondering who the devil she was and what she'd been doing watching him.

He'd be coming soon. She was certain of that.

A shiver crept up her arms, a mixture of tension and anticipation. Her skin felt sticky and itchy from crawling around in the cattails, and her hair had dried into a mass of stiff curls. She needed a shower badly, but she'd phoned in an urgent message to Margaret and couldn't risk missing a return call. She would want to know what had happened this afternoon, though Cara had already decided that certain minor details were unimportant and could be left out. One, that Ian had tied her up, and two, that he'd kissed her.

Touching her fingers to her lips, she remembered the press of his mouth against hers, the hot, though brief, brush of his tongue over her own. Killian Shawnessy was much more than she'd bargained for.

A hell of a lot more.

Of course, she knew that the only reason he'd kissed her was to stifle her scream, but somehow that didn't seem to ease the persistent tingling in her lips. Nor did it erase the memory of his hard, muscled body pressed against hers, his hands on her skin. She remembered those hands now. Large and rough, as skillful as they were experienced. There'd been no movement wasted, no hesitation or uncertainty. Though it nearly killed her to admit it, she admired and respected that.

It also made her mad as hell.

She'd learned how to handle herself from the time she was a little girl. With four big brothers, she'd had two choices: submit or assert. And since submission had never been her style, throughout her childhood she'd endured daily altercations with at least one of her siblings. Except Gabe. At thirty-five, he was the oldest, and had always been the one who'd saved her from serious injury when things got out of hand, dried her tears when frustration took over and she'd been reduced to that despicable female trait of crying.

The year following her parents' death when she was sixteen had been the hardest, but he'd been there for her then, too. Especially then, even though at twenty-four he suddenly had a family to hold together, as well as support. With three younger, headstrong brothers and a rebellious teenage sister, it hadn't been easy, but he'd managed, and somehow they'd all survived to become closer to each other than ever before.

She had the urge to call Gabe now, just to hear his voice. His soft, deep tone had always calmed her, and she could certainly use a little calming right now. Ian had shaken her self-confidence, not to mention her pride, and though she never would have admitted that—or what had happened— to anyone, not even Gabe, she could vent her annoyance on the phone in some meaningless nonrelated complaint and never once mention the name Killian Shawnessy.

In spite of her irritation with the man, she smiled slowly, remembering the look of astonishment on his face when she'd walked casually out of the bathroom and into the living room. That look had been her only compensation for the humiliation he'd caused her. She imagined that her heel digging into his foot had left a bruise, as well, but it served him right. How dare he tie her up and toss her in the bathtub!

But why had he done that? she wondered. The information she'd collected on him showed him to be an ordinary enough kind of guy: he owned a small business in Washington, D.C., manufacturing cellular phones; four years in the military, though that stint had ended ten years ago; no wife, no kids; and he lived in a one bedroom apartment in Maryland and drove a four-year-old Ford Explorer.

What reason would he have to be so suspicious of her? Why had he assumed she'd been lying when she'd told him she'd been bird watching? And why would he think anyone was watching him?

He had an edge to him, Cara thought. She recognized it. It was the same kind of edge her brother Lucian had. It was wild, reckless at times, but always contained, always just below the surface. Until something, or someone, brought it out.

Something told her there was more to Killian Shawnessy than met the eye. And whatever that something was, she intended to find out.

For now she'd wait. And while she was waiting, there was no reason not to enjoy the scenery.

She breathed in the scent of pine and damp leaves that drifted on the evening breeze. It had finally cooled down, and the air was comfortable, fresh and soft from the storm. Crickets came to life with their rhythmic night music, and bullfrogs joined in as background chorus.

This was as far from the city as a person could get, Cara thought, letting herself relax against the porch rail. No bumper-to-bumper traffic, no police sirens, no screaming arguments from the married couple in the apartment next to hers.

The quiet was wonderful, she told herself. Exactly what she needed.

It was going to drive her crazy.

She needed sound. Horns honking, the pounding beat of rock and roll, the blare of a television set. She'd been raised with noise, lots of it, and loud. She needed it to unwind, especially after a day like the one she'd had. But there was no TV, not even a radio in the cabin, and she'd have to settle for crickets and frogs.

A shower would help, and she decided to risk a quick

one. She figured she had at least another hour before Shawnessy showed up, and it would be easier to face him if she were clean and dressed in something other than military fatigues. A suit of armor, maybe.

She jumped at the sound of the phone ringing from inside the cabin, then hurried to answer it, locking the door securely behind her. She doubted a simple lock would keep Shawnessy out, but it might give her an extra couple of seconds to compose herself when he finally showed up. She almost laughed out loud at that thought. She'd had more than an hour and she wasn't ready to face the man. A couple of seconds would hardly matter.

She grabbed the phone on the third ring. "Hello?"

"Cara?" Margaret's voice was heavy with concern. "Are you all right, dear? Peter and I were worried when you didn't call earlier."

"I'm fine," she replied, though that wasn't completely truthful. "But I'm afraid there's been a little change in our plans."

Tanner's Tavern was dark and smoky. The gravelly wail of a country-western singer poured from a corner jukebox, while a pinball competition brought whoops and hollers from three men crowded around the clanging, lights-flashing machines at the back of the bar.

Lucas Blackhawk was bent over the cue ball, eyes narrowed while he set up his shot.

"Hey, Lucas." Nick casually chalked his cue on the opposite side of the table. "Did I mention that Ian was entertaining a beautiful woman in his cabin when I stopped by this afternoon?"

Lucas pitched forward, miscued and sank the cue ball. He glanced up sharply from the pool table. "*What* did you say?"

Ian tightened his hand around the cue stick he held and did his best to ignore the two sets of dark eyes focused on him. He'd known it was coming, of course. He'd been waiting for Nick to razz him about this afternoon ever since Lucas walked in thirty minutes ago. Ian was only surprised Nick had waited so long, but realized that he'd been waiting until Lucas was about to sink the game ball. Five bucks was five bucks, after all.

And now he'd never hear the end of it.

"A woman," Nick repeated. "As in female. As in drop-dead gorgeous. As in *hot*."

Ian moved to rack the balls, thought about slipping the wooden triangle over Nick's head and twisting. "Shut up, Santos."

Lucas straightened slowly and lifted one brow. "No kidding. So who is she?"

Ian knew they wouldn't go away if he ignored them, and besides, from past experience, he knew that the more evasive he was, the more curious they would be.

"No one you know." Ian scooped up the balls and dropped them into the rack. "She's on vacation, renting the cabin next to mine, and we ran into each other by the lake."

Nick leaned closer to Lucas. "He tried to get rid of me before she came out of the bathroom dripping wet."

Both brows raised now, Lucas stared at Ian. "Dripping wet?"

"We got caught in the storm," Ian said through clenched teeth. "She was drying off in the bathroom, that's all. She was fully clothed, for God's sake."

She had been fully clothed, Ian recalled, but her tank top had been tight over her full breasts, and she would have won a wet-T-shirt contest hands down. He forced the image from his mind, replaced it with the memory of her crushing her boot into his foot. It still throbbed.

Nick grinned. "She called him honey and darling."

Lucas's jaw went slack. "Ian's only been in town three days and he's already got himself a woman in his little mountain hideaway? You're putting me on."

Nick raised three fingers. "Scout's honor. Her name's Cara Sinclair. Blond hair, green eyes and a body that would make you—"

"Shut *up,* Santos," Ian warned. "And for a man who's getting married, you sure noticed a hell of a lot."

"A beautiful woman walks out of your bathroom and I'm not supposed to notice?" Nick leaned on his cue stick and gave a snort of disbelief. "Besides, I had to pay attention. Lucas wasn't there to share in the moment, and I figured he'd want details."

"Lucas has better things to do than listen to you yammer on about something that was nothing." Ian moved around the table to break. They weren't going to let this drop, he thought irritably. One more reason to dislike Miss Cara Sinclair.

"I haven't got anything better to do," Lucas said. "Julianna went with Maggie for their final fittings on their dresses, and they took the twins." Lucas grinned at Ian. "So she really called you honey?"

Ian broke hard and the balls exploded against the table's cushions. "Both of you can either put a sock in it and play pool, or I can leave and you two sweethearts can bat your eyes at each other and fantasize some more about my love life."

"He's jealous because she recognized me," Nick whispered loudly to Lucas. "She told me she's a fan of mine, and that she thinks I'm amazing."

"That does it." Ian threw his cue on the table, as annoyed with his friends as he was with himself for letting them get to him. "I've got better things to do than stand around here playing games with you girls."

"I'll bet you do," Nick said cheerfully. "And don't worry, I'll call before I stop by next time, lover boy."

Ian's response was simple and earthy, and Nick merely laughed. Ian decided he'd let them get it out of their system without him around. He stomped out of the bar into the parking lot toward the truck Nick had loaned him to drive for the two weeks he was visiting. The pickup was old, the paint worn, but the engine had been rebuilt. From a stop light he could leave a Porsche behind, reading his license plate.

He tightened his fingers around the steering wheel, revved the engine, then spun dirt and gravel coming out of the parking lot. He enjoyed the power of the machine under his hands. She took the curves like a dream, and by the time he reached the main dirt road that led to the lake, he felt in control again. Something he hadn't felt since that Sinclair woman walked out of his bathroom this afternoon.

He pulled off the dirt road onto a long driveway, shut off the headlights and cut the engine as he neared the cabin.

He needed one thing, and one thing only, from Miss Cara Sinclair—the truth. He wasn't leaving until he got it.

Three

Cara washed her hair twice, then dumped half a bottle of conditioner on the tangled mess, letting it soak in while she scoured her body with a liquid raspberry gel squeezed into a puffy ball of nylon. Even a practical girl deserved a few luxuries, she thought, sighing with pleasure as the hot water rinsed away the grime and sweat of her afternoon encounter with Ian. She knew better than to let herself relax under the invigorating spray; as it was, she'd taken too much time already, and regretfully, couldn't risk a long, leisurely shower. But even a few minutes was better than none, and at least she'd be clean.

And she'd also be able to think straight again, something she'd had trouble with since her first tangle with Ian in the cattails. It still irked her that he'd surprised her as he had, that he'd sneaked up so quietly, so smoothly, and overpowered her. Her pride was wounded, true, but more than that, he'd piqued her curiosity. She couldn't let go of the feeling that there was something amiss with the man, something that went well beneath the surface. And the more she thought about it, about him—which was constantly—the more curious she became.

Still, she wasn't here to be *curious* about Ian, she told herself, washing the last of the soapy suds from her skin. She'd come here to find him. The fact that he'd found *her*, as well, was inconvenient, but still didn't change anything.

Quickly she rinsed her hair, then turned off the water and grabbed one of the two white towels she'd tossed over the shower curtain bar. Bending at the waist, she wrapped her hair in the soft towel, then reached for the second one.

It wasn't there.

She was reaching around the shower curtain to retrieve the fallen towel when it appeared in front of her face.

"Looking for this?"

Ian!

With a small squeak, Cara snatched the towel from his hand while she darted back behind the shower curtain and covered herself. Damn, damn, *damn!* He'd gone through *two* locked doors. "Get out of here!"

No reply. "Ian?" Still no response.

After another long, silent moment, she peeked around the shower curtain. Arms folded, he stood with his back against the closed bathroom door. Steam swirled around his long, muscular body. He'd changed into a black T-shirt that stretched tight over his broad chest. His eyes were dark and narrowed as he met her gaze, and she swallowed hard. He looked like the devil himself.

"Mr. Shawnessy, would you please remove yourself from this bathroom?" she asked tightly.

He slowly raised one dark brow. "What happened to 'honey' and 'darling'?"

Since he obviously had the upper hand here, she'd humor

him. For the moment, at least. "All right." She sucked in a breath. "*Darling,* would you please get out of here?"

He pressed his lips together thoughtfully. "No."

He was laughing at her! She could see the amusement in his eyes. The shower curtain twisted in her clenched fist. She'd murder him. As soon as she had some clothes on.

"Ian," she mewed sweetly through clenched teeth. "*Honey,* would you *please* leave this bathroom and wait for me in the living room while I get dressed?"

Dropping his arms, he pushed away from the door and moved toward her. She swallowed the gasp in her throat, refusing to let him see her fear, but preparing herself to fight him off if necessary. She clutched the shower curtain tightly to her, but held his gaze as he moved in front of her. Her breath caught when he reached out and captured one long strand of hair that had escaped from under the towel on her head. His knuckles skimmed her shoulders while he gently rubbed the wet hair between his thumb and forefinger.

He leaned close, and she felt his warm breath fan over her cheek. "Call me 'sweetheart', and I'll leave."

He was playing a game with her, Cara knew that. And as much as she wanted to kill him for it, she also found it exciting, like nothing she'd ever experienced before. She stood naked in the shower, with only a thin, plastic shower curtain and towel separating her from this stranger, a man she'd never laid eyes on until a few hours ago. Her heart pounded furiously; she could barely catch her breath. Her wet skin felt hot and tight.

"Sweetheart," she whispered, still refusing to break contact with his eyes.

Immediately she wanted to snatch the single word back. The amusement she'd seen in his eyes only moments ago darkened to something else entirely. Something dangerous and primitive. It felt as if the tiny room were closing in on them. Steam swirled around their bodies like a wispy veil of desire. He still held her hair between his fingers, and she felt connected to him through the wet strands. When he brushed his knuckles over her collarbone, she shivered.

"Tell me how you got out of those ropes," he said softly.

She kept her eyes steady, in spite of the fear slithering up her spine. "Are you going to tie me up again?"

He smiled slowly. "Not unless you ask me to."

Frowning, she lifted her chin at him. "Don't flatter yourself.... I was the Houdini act in my neighborhood amateur talent show when I was growing up. My record for escape was two minutes, twenty-seven seconds. I won three years running. Now will you *please* get out of my bathroom?"

He hesitated, then released her hair and stepped away. "You've got five minutes. If you haven't come out, I'll be back."

The breath she'd been holding slowly escaped when he closed the door behind him. She stared for several long seconds.

Five minutes.

His ultimatum seeped into her numb brain, and she sprang into action, not even bothering to dry her still-damp skin before she dragged on a pair of blue jeans and a white button-up shirt. She yanked the towel from her hair and tugged a comb through the tangled mess, thankful that she'd used conditioner. She could escape rope knots any day, but the knots in her hair were something else all together.

Blast the man for catching her off guard like that!

Hands on his hips, Ian paced the small living room. He had no idea exactly what had just taken place in the bathroom, but he knew he didn't like it one little bit. He'd intended to rattle the woman, but all he'd ended up doing was rattling himself. He'd been messing with her when he told her to call him sweetheart, but when she had, and her voice had sounded so breathless, all he'd wanted to do was kiss her. And when her eyes got all soft and dewy when he'd touched her hair, Lord help him, he nearly had.

Damn if he still didn't want to kiss her.

But he also wanted to throttle her. Not only because she'd been lying to him and spying on him, but because she was so casual about it. She could at least have the decency to appear just a little afraid. A strange man standing in her bathroom while she's taking a shower and she didn't even scream or cry.

Not that he'd actually seen anything. He'd only been there a moment before he handed her the towel, and she'd been behind the shower curtain the entire time. For all he knew, she had a gun back there, and if he'd tried anything, she would have blown his head off.

No, he didn't think she had a gun, nor did he think she intended to kill him. She'd been watching him, that was all he knew. And he intended to find out why.

Right about—he glanced at his watch, followed the second hand as it swept up to the twelve—now.

He was turning toward the bathroom when she came out, dressed in jeans and a white, untucked, buttoned shirt rolled to her elbows. She'd combed her hair away from her face and the wet ends lay heavy on her shoulders and down her back. Her skin was flushed from her shower, her cheeks rosy and green eyes bright.

She brought the fresh, clean smell of wet raspberries with her from the shower. It filled the room, made him want to breathe deeper and drag the scent fully into his senses. Still not completely recovered from touching her in the bathroom, he decided it would be best to keep his distance.

"We've got to stop meeting like this, Mr. Shawnessy." She tossed him a smile. "People are going to talk."

"Thanks to you, they already are." He ignored the drops of water sliding down her neck into the vee of her shirt and kept his gaze carefully locked with hers. "Nick's a regular Gertrude Gossip."

"I didn't think it would benefit either one of us for me to drag him into our—" she hesitated "—situation."

"Tell me, Miss Sinclair, what exactly is our *situation?*"

"That's what we're going to talk about." She padded toward the kitchen in her bare feet. "But I'm starving and we have to eat first. Are you hungry?"

Incredulous, Ian watched her walk away. Cara Sinclair was one cool woman. In spite of himself, she fascinated him. And anyway, he thought, turning on his heels to follow her, he *was* hungry. He'd left Tanner's before ordering food, and he hadn't eaten anything since the ham sandwich he'd made around noon, exactly eight hours ago.

But even if he had eaten, the smells emanating from the kitchen were so incredibly mouthwatering, he would have been tempted, anyway. His stomach grumbled as he drew in a lungful of the delicious aroma.

Cara stood at the stove with a wooden spoon in her hand, stirring a large pot. The back of her shirt was wet from her hair, nearly making the fabric see-through, and he realized she wasn't wearing a bra. The woman was as mouthwatering as the smell of food and equally tempting, he thought reluctantly, which triggered another response from his body, lower than his stomach.

Annoyed at his unwanted reaction to her, he looked away and noticed she'd set the small kitchen table for two. He glanced back sharply at her. "Expecting company?"

"I knew you'd be here sooner or later," she said with a shrug. "I hate to eat alone."

He didn't. In fact, he preferred it. He'd had a couple of steady relationships over the years, but his job kept him away for long periods of time, and even the most patient woman had her limits. He'd gotten used to living alone. It was easier—fewer complications.

But this woman was intent on playing out this little scenario her way, so he sat. For now he'd let her have her way. Short of violence—which he still hadn't ruled out—it seemed to be the quickest way to find out what he wanted to know. And if what she was cooking tasted half as good as it smelled, the wait just might be worth it.

She set two bowls of steaming chili on the table. "Dig in."

He hesitated. "How do I know it's not laced with arsenic?"

She smiled. "You don't."

He decided she didn't look like a murderer and scooped up a big bite. It was all he could do not to moan with pleasure as the spicy concoction rolled over his tongue.

He suddenly felt ravenous.

He was on his second bite when she moved back to the stove and, using a kitchen towel as a hot pad, pulled a tray of corn muffins from the oven. Plucking them carefully into a small wicker basket, she then scooped another bowl of chili and set everything on the table.

"Good?" She sat beside him.

He shrugged. "It's all right."

Scooting her chair in closer, she grinned at him. "It's better than all right, Flash. I didn't win the Bloomfield All-County Chili Bake-off two years running for nothing. Consider yourself lucky."

He reached for a muffin. "I've been spied on, had my

vacation interrupted, bruised and nearly lost the ability to ever have children. Of all the things I consider myself, Miss Sinclair—'' he broke open the muffin and slathered it with butter ''—lucky is not one of them.''

"I apologize for all that. You shouldn't have sneaked up on me like you did.'' She took a muffin herself and nibbled on it. "But you shouldn't have tied me up, either. That was incredibly rude.''

"Sweetheart, if you think *that* was rude, you ain't seen nothing yet.'' He was getting tired of bantering with her. And now that his stomach was nearly satisfied, there were questions he wanted answered. "Cut to the chase, darlin'. I want to know who you are, who you *really* are, and I want to know who sent you here.''

With a sigh Cara got up and retrieved two cans of soda from the refrigerator. She handed him one, then popped the top of her own and sat back down. "My name really is Cara Sinclair, just like my driver's license stated. Give or take a pound, I won't say which way, my weight is also accurate. So is my height and address.''

Cara knew this wasn't exactly what Ian meant when he wanted to know who she was, but she was getting to all that, and since she had no idea how he was going to accept what she was about to say, she hardly felt that she should just blurt it out.

"I moved to Philadelphia from Bloomfield County almost two years ago and took a position with Myers and Smith, they're—''

"Security specialists.'' Ian popped the lid of his soda, took a swig. "High-level stuff. Wealthy clients and large corporations are their main clientele.''

She nodded, but couldn't help wondering why a man who owned a small company manufacturing cellular phones would be familiar with Myers and Smith. They didn't exactly advertise in the phone book. "That's right. They brought me into their research department. I'd been working for an insurance company in Bloomfield, tracking down addresses of people who'd filed questionable claims. It was boring, tedious work, but I was good at it. When I saw the ad for Myers and Smith, I jumped at the chance to move into something more interesting."

Ian's legs were long, and it was impossible not to bump knees with him under the small table. He didn't seem to notice, but the repeated contact was making her edgy. The more she told herself to ignore him, the more aware of him, of his size and his closeness, she became.

"They hired me—" she cleared her throat when it cracked slightly "—and then I found out the work was just as boring as my old job. Stuck in a cubicle all day, basically doing the same thing I'd done at the insurance company. Every training position I'd apply for that sounded interesting, whether it was surveillance or internal security or even alarm setting-up, always went to a man."

"Are you going to get to the point sometime soon?" Ian asked, pushing his empty bowl aside. "Or do I have to time this story with a calendar?"

Cara pressed her lips tightly together, but refused to let Ian's impatience sway her. "Fourteen months ago, a multimillion-dollar accounting firm in Philadelphia, Muldoon and Associates, hired Myers and Smith to quietly flush out an embezzler. For obvious reasons it was important that the investigation be kept quiet. After two months, the field agents hadn't found a thing. The firm's owner, Margaret Muldoon, had turned over company management to her nephew, Peter Muldoon, three years earlier, and he became increasingly angry with the investigation and its lack of progress."

Ian rolled his eyes. "I know the feeling."

Ignoring him, Cara took a bite of chili and intentionally chewed slowly before she went on. "Without authorization, I followed up on the banking and spending habits of the employees who weren't suspect. Details are my specialty and I dug deeper, followed every possible lead, and some not so possible."

"And you found your man," Ian said, pointing his can of soda at her. "Or woman, let's say, just to keep the story equal opportunity."

"It was a man. Turned out he was Peter Muldoon's secretary. He'd been with the company for over twenty years, a quiet, hardworking man no one would have ever suspected. Myself included, but the evidence was overwhelming."

She shook her head and sighed. "Unfortunately, when we got too close, the man ended his own life. None of the money was recovered."

"So you saved the day and were rewarded justly," Ian said dryly.

"I was fired for not following procedure."

He lifted a brow. "That so?"

"I was packing up my things in my cubicle," Cara went on smoothly, "when the most elegant, sophisticated silver-hair woman appeared at my desk."

"Don't tell me." Ian mocked her. "Your fairy godmother, come to rescue you from sweeping ashes and take you to the ball."

In spite of her exasperation, Cara couldn't help but smile. "Close. It was Margaret Muldoon herself. She'd come by to personally thank me. She didn't know that I'd been canned and was furious when I told her, insisted she'd have my job back immediately or there'd be hell to pay."

"Feisty old broad," Ian murmured and found himself reaching for another muffin.

Cara chuckled softly. "You don't know the half of it. Anyway, I thanked her for her concern, then turned her down. Told her that she'd done me a favor. She insisted on taking me to lunch, then made me an offer I couldn't refuse."

"The fairy godmother turns into a mafia godfather. Is there a horse involved here?" Ian brushed the crumbs off his hands and looked at her blandly. "And even more important, is there a point to all this, or are you trying to kill me through sheer boredom?"

"There is a point, Mr. Shawnessy," Cara said tightly. "And I'd have been there already if you didn't keep interrupting with sarcastic comments."

He pressed his lips together and leaned close—close enough she could smell his masculine scent, a scent that stirred her own femininity, reminded her of earlier in the day when that strong, hard mouth had been crushed firmly against her own.

She snatched up their empty bowls and moved to the sink, poured soap on a sponge, then turned on the water. "Margaret offered me the money to start a security company of my own, no strings attached," she continued while rinsing the bowls. "I turned her down, but at her persistence, finally told her that I would accept a loan, but only on one condition, that she become my partner. She refused at first, but I was just as persistent as she was. Hence the birth of Sinclair and Muldoon Enterprises. Margaret runs the office two days a week and keeps the books."

Ian gave a snort of laughter. "You're trying to tell me that this woman, the owner of a multimillion-dollar company, answers your business phone?"

"*Our* business phone," Cara said over her shoulder. "And that's exactly what I'm telling you. Her position with Muldoon and Associates had become more figurehead than productive. Until she came to work with me, she spent her time at ladies' luncheons and charity teas. She was bored and lonely.''

''I'll just bet her children love you,'' Ian muttered thoughtfully.

''Her only son has been dead for thirty-three years. Her only brother has been gone for five years.'' Cara rinsed the bowls, then set them on the dish. ''Her nephew, Peter, dotes on her, but he's busy running Muldoon and Associates.''

Cara glanced over her shoulder, watched as Ian rose and stepped toward the sink. Toward her. Cara turned off the water and was reaching for a towel when he moved behind her and placed his long arms on either side of her, effectively pinning her against the counter.

She felt his chest against her back, the press of his thighs against her own. She turned slowly and faced him, realized her mistake immediately when her breasts brushed against his chest. Since she was wearing only the thin cotton shirt, the contact was electrifying. Heart pounding, she leaned back, forced herself to look into his eyes.

He stared down at her. She felt weak and hot and ridiculously aroused. When he pressed in closer, she gasped, realized that he was aroused, as well.

This wasn't going at all the way she'd planned.

''Story time is over,'' he said harshly. ''I want the bottom line now. *Why the hell were you watching me?*''

She drew in a slow, deep breath, swallowed and lifted her face to his. ''We had to be sure. Margaret felt that if she had a picture of you, then she would know.''

His gaze narrowed, his eyes turned black as the darkness outside. ''Know what?''

''That you are her grandson.''

Four

Ian blinked twice, then very carefully, very slowly said, "*What* did you say?"

"Ian, come sit down."

He felt the pressure of her hand on his chest and ignored it. "You're telling me that my *grandmother,* a woman named Margaret Muldoon, sent you here to find me?"

"Please…"

Her voice softened, but there was an edge of desperation there, as well, Ian noted. He realized that he'd pressed her tightly against the counter, that their bodies were touching intimately. He might have indulged himself and prolonged the contact if she hadn't just laid a bombshell on him.

On a curse, he moved away and shook his head. "You're good, Blondie. Real good. You almost had me there. Now I want the truth."

"I'm telling you the truth." She straightened, placed both hands on the counter behind her and drew in a slow breath. "Margaret Muldoon, Philadelphia socialite, owner and chairman of the board of a multimillion-dollar a year accounting firm, is your grandmother. Now will you please sit down?"

He did, but only because the kitchen was too small for him to pace effectively. He glanced at his watch, then folded his arms and stared at her. "Start talking."

With a sigh, she dragged one hand through her damp hair. "Thirty-three years ago you were abandoned as a newborn on the steps of St. Matthew's Seminary in Wolf River, with no clue to your mother's or father's identity. You were adopted two weeks later by Joseph and Kathleen Shawnessy and legally became Killian O'Neil Shawnessy. Your father was a crop duster, and on Sundays he would fly you and your mother on pleasure trips. One Sunday when you were nine years old, they were both killed when their plane went down. You had the chicken pox that day, and they'd left you home with a baby-sitter."

He held the pain of that memory to himself, kept his face impassive as he stared blankly back at her. "All a matter of record."

"You spent the next nine years bouncing around foster homes," she went on. "Even did six months at the Wolf River Home for Boys for breaking your history teacher's nose when you were thirteen."

He smiled at that memory. Punching out that slime bucket Thompson had been worth every day at the Home. "Which only proves I have a violent nature. If you don't get to the point soon, you're going to see it."

The patient look she shot him made him want to shake her. "You joined the Marines two years after you graduated high school, completed four years, then started a cellular phone company in Washington, D.C. You never married, have no children of public record and you rent a one-bedroom apartment in Maryland.''

"You did a lot of digging, Blondie," he said dryly. "If I wasn't so annoyed that it was my personal life you've stuck your nose into, I'd be impressed."

"Like I said, details are my specialty. I make a point to pay close attention."

He might tell her that he was paying attention to a few of her details, as well, such as the damp spots making her blouse almost see-through, and the curve of her long legs in her snug jeans.

But he'd rather not be distracted at the moment, so he forced his attention to her eyes, noticed the smug satisfaction in her green gaze. She might not look so smug if he told her that she'd uncovered no more about his current life than anyone else with a personal computer and telephone could have done. Anything else would require a level-four security pass. And that, he was certain, Miss Cara Sinclair didn't have.

He was almost beginning to enjoy this little game. It had been a long time since a woman had intrigued him. And it had been a hell of a lot longer since he'd felt an attraction as intense as the one she evoked in him. There was something about her eyes that fascinated him. They changed color with her moods. When she was angry they shone like green fire. After he'd kissed her, they'd turned smoky. A few moments ago, when he'd had her pinned against the sink, they'd softened to the color of a spring meadow. He'd wanted her, just as much as he was certain she'd wanted him, and it had taken a will of iron not to strip down her jeans, lift her onto that counter and take her.

The thought alone aroused him, but he forced it back down. "How 'bout you tell me something I don't already know, Sherlock."

"All right." She tossed her head back and sent the ends of her hair over her shoulders. "Your father, Margaret's only child, was Richard Muldoon. Your mother, Richard's girlfriend, was Fiona Francisco DeCarlo. They were in love, but your grandfather, Daniel Muldoon, forbade them to marry. When Fiona became pregnant with you, they were going to run away, but your father was struck by a car when he was crossing the street outside of their home in Philadelphia. That was thirty-three years ago. Six months before you were born."

He didn't believe any of it. He wondered briefly if the Agency was responsible for all this, inventing this ridiculous story to test his reaction, to see if this woman could gain his confidence and convince him to reveal sensitive information.

Or worse, if she wasn't from the Agency, if someone else had sent her.... He didn't like the thought of that at all. Didn't want to consider what he'd have to do if she turned out to be someone other than who she said she was.

He leaned back in his chair, kept his expression bland and his tone bored. "So my grandparents paid Fiona to give me up, and now, thirty-three years later they're having an acute guilt attack and want to claim me as their own."

Cara shook her head. "Fiona disappeared after your father died. Margaret searched for her, even though your grandfather disapproved, but she came up empty-handed. Four months later, your mother sent a letter and said that you had died in childbirth. Margaret didn't believe her, but Fiona never came back to Philadelphia and left no trace of her whereabouts. Margaret searched for you for years, even after your grandfather died, but never found anything to give her hope."

"Until you came along." Ian kept his gaze carefully

locked with hers. If she was lying, she was damn good, he thought.

Her sigh was heavy as she pushed away from the counter. "I ran computer checks on every member of Fiona's family, extended family and friends, everyone she might have associated with. Then I ran checks on every hospital within a hundred miles of each person, at the same time checking the birth records within a two week period of when Fiona was due to deliver. Out of the twenty-five hospitals, there were three hundred live births, four still-born. I followed up on every one, until I narrowed my search down to four possibilities, none of them stillborn. Out of those four, I was finally left with one possibility, a child born in Ridgeville, a small town fifty miles east of Wolf River. The family couldn't be traced, and the mother had apparently lied on the birth certificate."

Ian lifted his hands in mock admiration. "So naturally that has to mean I'm Fiona's child. I'm sure no other un-married mother, especially thirty-three years ago, ever lied on a birth certificate."

"I realize that." There was an edge of irritation in her voice. "It turned out Fiona's cousin, Angela, a second cousin actually, lived in Ridgeville. Still lives in Ridgeville. I went to see her."

Eyes narrowed, he glanced up sharply.

Cara moved to the table and sat beside him, leaning in close. There was an excitement in her eyes, Ian noted, a brightness which made them sharper, the green more intense.

"Angela told me that Fiona had been living with her for six months." Cara's voice had a breathless quality to it. "She drove Fiona to the hospital when she went into labor, checked her into Ridgeville hospital under a fake name, then checked her out two days later when she left with her baby, a healthy, dark-haired boy.''

Ian waited, suddenly aware he'd been holding his breath.

"The next morning," Cara said softly, "Angela drove Fiona and the baby to Wolf River. In the early hours of the morning on April 29, she wrapped her three-day-old son in a white blanket embroidered with tiny blue roses, then placed him in a basket and left him on the steps of St. Matthew's Seminary.''

Cara leaned closer, placed her hand on his arm. Her fingers were warm and smooth. "That baby was you, Ian.''

Ian heard the distant, heavy sound of his own heartbeat. The twenty-ninth was the same day he'd been left at the seminary. And somewhere, in a box on a closet shelf in his apartment, was a white blanket embroidered with blue roses.

No one knew about the blanket, except maybe Father MacRoy, the old priest who'd found him that morning. And Father MacRoy had been dead for twenty years. Even the police report simply described the blanket as white.

And what no one knew but him, Ian thought dimly, no one at all, was that under one tiny blue flower, so small it was never noticed by anyone else but himself, were the initials F. F. D.

Fiona Francisco DeCarlo.

Growing up, how many times had he taken that blanket down and touched those initials, wondered what they meant, who they belonged to?

How many times had he wondered why?

But that was years ago. It might have mattered then, but not now. Some things were just better left alone.

And that's what he wanted. To be left alone.

"Well, blondie, it's been real." His blood felt thick and slow as he rose from his chair. "Thanks for the food and entertainment, but I've got an early-morning date with a fish.''

Cara stood, her expression incredulous. "Ian, after what I just told you, how can you walk away?"

He didn't just want to walk. He wanted to run. On an impulse, he pulled her into his arms and kissed her hard. To his surprise, she didn't resist. But she didn't respond, either.

When he finally released her, she stumbled back, her eyes wide, her lips parted and moist. He wanted to kiss her again, he realized, and knew it was time to get the hell out.

"Walking away obviously runs in the family," he said flatly. "Tell Margaret thanks for the thought, but I'm not interested."

With that he turned and left.

The lake was blue and calm at seven the next morning; the air cool and still, filled with the sound of birdsong and the scent of pine. Rocks and pine needles crunched under her boots as Cara followed the path between her cabin and Ian's, and from the low branch of a pine tree, a large gray squirrel chattered irritably at her intrusion.

Amazing how that squirrel reminded her of Ian.

She shifted the bag of groceries in her arms and frowned at the tail-twitching rodent, decided if she could deal with four bullheaded brothers, she could deal with one Killian Shawnessy.

She'd had a long, sleepless night to think about Ian's reaction to what she'd told him. Of course he'd be angry, she'd reasoned. His mother had abandoned him. He had every right to be angry. She could certainly understand that.

What she didn't understand was his cold, calm acceptance of the information, or why he hadn't at least asked questions. Not even one. Outwardly he gave the impression he wasn't interested, but when he'd kissed her, she'd felt the emotion churning inside him, emotions that went deeper than lust.

That kiss had been another reason she'd spent a sleepless night. Every time she'd closed her eyes, every time she'd started to drift off, she'd felt the power of that kiss, the desire on her lips. He'd caught her off guard—again—and it frightened her that she'd nearly given in to him.

Lord help her, she'd wanted to.

At the edge of the woods Cara paused, then spotted two rowboats out on the lake. The father and son she'd seen at the cabin rental office in town were in one boat at the far end of the lake, Ian was in the other.

His line was cast, his back to her, yet somehow she had the feeling he knew she was there. Very little got past this man, in spite of the bored attitude he wore most of the time. Occasionally, and each time only for the briefest of moments, his eyes would give him away. There was a clarity in those deep, dark orbs. A sharp-edged intelligence that astounded her.

"Good morning."

She jumped at the unexpected greeting from behind her, then turned. A good-looking dark-haired man and a slender, pretty redhead were walking up the path, their arms around each other's waist. They both smiled at her.

She smiled back. "Morning."

"Bob and Pamela Waters." The man stuck out his hand. "Cabin two."

"Cara Sinclair. Cabin four." Cara took the man's hand, then the woman's. When they immediately hugged each other again, it was easy to figure out who they were. "You must be the honeymoon couple that the woman at the rental office mentioned."

Pamela wiggled a wedding ring. "Four whole days."

"But who's counting?" Bob said, then they smiled at each other, one of those I-love-you-so-much, newlywed smiles that most people thought were cute. Cara wasn't one of those people.

"Isn't it beautiful here?" Pamela hugged her husband. "Bobby and I live in Dallas. We've decided we're going to come here every year for our anniversary. Didn't we, baby?"

"Bobby baby" rewarded his bride with a kiss. "That's right, sweetcakes."

Baby and sweetcakes on an empty stomach was almost too much for Cara. She smiled tightly. "That's great."

"How 'bout you?" Bob asked. "Where you from?"

She glanced at the lake. Ian hadn't moved. "Philadelphia."

Pamela's big blue eyes got bigger. "Goodness. What brings you all the way here?"

"I'm trying to get over my second divorce." Cara watched as Ian reeled up a wiggling trout. "I've been a little stressed since my husband ran away with my sister. My therapist thought the solitude here would be a good idea."

Bob and Pamela's smiles faded. "Oh dear, I'm so sorry," Pamela said awkwardly, then glanced at her husband. "Goodness, Bobby, the time just flies up here, doesn't it? Well, ah, we've got to be off now, Miss Sinclair, but we'll, ah, see you around."

Feeling absolutely wicked, Cara waved as the couple turned and walked quickly away. "Enjoy your honeymoon," she called out.

They didn't look back, just kept walking.

Marriage was fine, Cara thought, watching them disappear when the path curved. She intended to try it someday herself. After she'd established her business and put her nest egg away. Of course, she'd have to find the right guy first, but that was a detail. An important one, but a detail nonetheless. She definitely wanted kids, too, so she knew she wouldn't wait too long.

But if her husband ever called her sweetcakes, she thought with a frown, he'd be sporting a black eye and sleeping on the couch for a long time.

She headed for Ian's cabin, let herself in the unlocked front door. Thirty minutes later, when he came into the cabin, she was frying potatoes, onions and bell peppers.

Without so much as glancing her way, he shrugged out of his jacket and moved to the kitchen sink.

"Good morning," she said cheerfully.

No response. He scrubbed his hands, splashed water on his face and reached for a towel.

Cara's heart jumped against her ribs at the sight of him. He had a rugged, wild look about him this morning. His faded jeans hugged his lean hips, and the red-plaid flannel shirt he'd rolled to his elbows gave him the rough-tough appearance of a lumberjack. His morning beard was dark; his hair, rumpled. He looked like he'd just tumbled out of bed.

She drew in a slow, deep breath, counted to three and reminded herself she was here to talk to him, not jump into that bed with him.

"I just brewed some coffee." She gestured to the pot. "I hope you like it strong."

He poured himself a cup, then leaned back against the counter and slid his gaze slowly over her. The white cotton T-shirt and jeans she had on were hardly provocative, but the intensity of his look burned, made her feel as if she were standing there naked.

"How do you like to eat your eggs?" Her fingers trembled as she reached for the carton on the counter.

"Alone," he said dryly and sipped his coffee.

She smiled at him. At least she had him talking. Sort of. "I promise I'll leave after we talk."

"We already talked. Which part of, 'I'm not interested, now go away,' don't you understand?"

She decided he was the hard-boiled type, but sunny-side-up was what he was going to get. She cut butter into a heated frying pan, then cracked three eggs into a bowl and dumped them in, too. They sizzled in the melting butter. "I can't just go away. How could I tell Margaret that you don't want to see her?"

"Easy. You say, 'He doesn't want to see you.'"

"She's your *grandmother*. Your family. That has to mean something to you."

He shook his head. "Lucas and Nick are my family. The only family I've known since I was nine years old. The only two people in the world I know I can count on, that I can trust. I don't need any more than that."

"At least give her a chance." Cara piled a plate with eggs and potatoes and set it on the table. "Come to Philadelphia with me. You can meet her and your cousin Peter, too."

He laughed at that, sat at the table and attacked his food. "Not a chance," he mumbled around a big bite of potatoes. "I'm here for a wedding, then I'm going home."

"After the wedding, then." She sat with her own plate of food.

"No."

"What could one day hurt?"

"No."

"I'll bet Nick and Lucas could convince you."

He glared at her and slowly lowered his fork. "If I want them to know about this, I'll tell them."

"All right, all right. I get the picture." She sighed with

exasperation. "Well, then, how are you going to explain me?"

"There's nothing to explain. My friends will mind their own business, unlike some people. And besides, you're going back to Philadelphia."

Her smile was slow and sweet. "I can't do that. I made a promise to Margaret. I always keep my promises."

One corner of his mouth tipped up as he reached out and took her chin in his hand. The look in his eyes seared her right down to her toes, and her breath caught as he brought his face close to hers.

"Here's a promise for you, too." The tone in his voice was laden with sexuality. "I'm going back out on the lake now. If you're still here when I get back, I'm going to do something we both want, and we'll both regret."

He released her, then pushed away from the table. "Get this through that pretty little head of yours—I'm not going back to Philadelphia. Not now. Not ever. Now stop bothering me."

He stomped out of the cabin, and once again Cara felt completely out of balance. Light-headed and unwound.

She let out a long, slow breath, and with shaking hands, quickly cleaned up. Her skin still burned where he'd touched her. The look in his eyes said it all, and she knew she'd better get out of there before he got back.

Five

He spent the next twenty-four hours in blissful silence. Fishing, reading, counting spiders on the front porch. An entire day of quiet, by himself. Exactly what he'd wanted, exactly what he'd asked for.

So why the hell was he so damn edgy?

It wasn't the bombshell that Blondie had laid on him the night before last. It was going to take some time to absorb what she'd told him about his parents and grandmother, and he wasn't sure how he felt about any of it.

If he felt anything.

He wasn't ready to accept any of her story as fact just yet, and until he looked into the matter himself, he had no intention of giving it more than minimal brain space.

But Cara Sinclair was another story. He'd given equal effort to putting her out of his mind, as well, and met with no success.

Blasted woman. He glanced out the kitchen window,

watching the woods, half expecting her to be hiding there, watching him. She wasn't, though. Even if he couldn't see her, he'd know if she was there. He'd *feel* it.

So what the hell *was* she up to?

And why the hell couldn't he get her off his mind?

Only because he didn't trust her, he told himself, and walked away from the window. He kept expecting her to pop up any minute, her green eyes smiling and that sassy little mouth yammering. A mouth he'd thought about well into his sleepless night.

Fortunately for her, she'd taken him seriously when he'd told her to leave after breakfast yesterday. If she'd been there when he'd come back, he would have dragged her straight to his bed—exactly where he'd wanted her since he'd tied her up in the cattails by the lake.

He sighed heavily and scrubbed a hand over his face. Damn, he must be one sick bastard.

He could understand wanting to take the woman to bed; he had a healthy appetite when it came to sex. What he couldn't understand was his preoccupation with her. Why she continually crept into his thoughts. She wasn't even his type, he thought irritably. She had the looks, all right, and she certainly had a body that wouldn't quit, but Washington was full of women who fit that bill.

Cara Sinclair was just too spontaneous, too enthusiastic and too damn trusting. She obviously hadn't spent much time in the real world.

Yanking on a jeans jacket, he stomped out of the cabin and climbed into the truck. He was meeting Lucas and Nick at the tailor's, where they had to be fitted for tuxedos, of all things. Nick owed him big time for this. The only thing Ian hated more than wearing a tuxedo was wearing a cast. And a cast was considerably more comfortable, not to mention considerably less ridiculous looking.

He drove down the dirt road that led by Cara's cabin, but only because it was the easiest route leading to the main road, he told himself. Her Jeep was gone, and he wondered if she'd finally given up and gone back to Philadelphia. Not that it mattered to him one way or the other. She could stay or hang around all she wanted, as long as she didn't bother him.

Except she did bother him. A lot.

Downshifting the truck, he pulled out onto the steep mountain road, found a hard-rock station on the radio, then cranked up the volume.

Maybe music could drown the woman out of his mind.

In spite of his need to flatten the accelerator, he slowed at the hairpin curve at Meadow View, the half way point down the mountain. It wasn't uncommon to come upon a deer in the road here, or occasionally a boulder that had tumbled down.

He rounded the curve and slammed on the brakes, though not for a deer or a boulder. It was Cara.

Her Jeep was sideways, half on the road, half off. She knelt behind one of the rear tires, and was peering underneath the car. At the sound of his truck pulling alongside hers, she glanced up, then stood.

Brushing off her hands, she stuck them into the front pockets of her jeans. Her pink cotton T-shirt was smudged with dust across her breasts, and he struggled to keep his eyes on her face.

She watched him approach, her manner contrite, almost demure, a side of her he hadn't seen before. The corners of her mouth tipped upward, a proper damsel-in-distress smile. Hesitant, but welcoming. Her cheeks were flushed, and her hair tumbled in soft curls around her face and shoulders.

Damn if she didn't look appealing, he thought, which only increased his irritation.

"Morning," she greeted him.

He nodded. "What's the problem?"

"Rear brakes locked up on me when I came around the curve." She pointed to the skid marks on the road. "Lucky for me I spun into the shoulder when I slammed on the brakes."

Damn lucky, Ian thought and hunkered down to look under the rear of the car. The rear brakes had locked up; he could still smell the smoke. The drop-off at this point in the mountain was high and straight down. If she hadn't spun sideways into the shoulder— Ten more feet, and the Jeep, with Cara in it, would have gone over the edge.

The image of her at the bottom of the cliff, still in the Jeep, had Ian's fists clenching.

Hands on her knees, she bent beside him. He caught her scent, raspberries again, felt the warmth of her skin radiate in velvet waves over his body. When her arm accidentally brushed his shoulder, he felt as if he'd been sucker punched. It took him a moment to catch him breath before he stood.

"I'm going to push it out of the road," he said more roughly than he intended. "Get in and steer."

She jumped into the driver's seat, and he dug his heels into the asphalt and pushed. The Jeep was barely off the road when a black Explorer whipped around the curve and spun directly toward them. He opened his mouth to yell for Cara to jump when the Explorer straightened, then slid to a halt.

Ian was swearing under his breath as the driver, a stocky, gray-haired man wearing a fishing cap, stepped out of the car.

"Good God, we almost hit you folks." The driver's voice held a mixture of apology and fear. "You all right?"

"Fine," Ian ground out, watched as the passenger, a twenty-something blond man in sunglasses, came around the car.

"Car trouble?" the driver asked.

Cara moved beside Ian. "Brakes."

"Name's Wexler. Bill Wexler." The driver held out his hand to Ian. "My son, Paul, and I are renting one of the cabins by the lake. Say—" Bill grinned at Cara "—you were in the rental office the day we got into town. Nice to see you again."

Cara smiled at Bill, but Ian's attention was directed at Paul, who was staring a little too long and a little too hard at Cara.

"Can we give you a lift?" Bill looked at Cara. "We were just going into town for supplies."

Cara opened her mouth, but Ian took a step forward and shook his head. "Thanks, but I've got the situation under control."

Ian felt Cara's eyes on him, but for once the woman knew when to keep quiet. Even after the two men had returned to their car and driven away, she was still staring in stunned silence.

He turned abruptly and faced her. "What?"

"You had the perfect opportunity to get rid of me just now. But you didn't."

When a soft smile touched her tempting lips, he felt his body respond. Grinding his teeth, he turned on his heels and headed for his truck.

"Don't make me wish I had," he said and climbed into the cab.

"They'll have to come in from Dallas, but if I order the parts now—" Walt, the barrel-chested, hulk-size mechanic at Gibson Automotive, wiped his large hands on a rag, then shoved it into his back pocket "—well, I can probably have her ready for you tomorrow afternoon. Day after tomorrow at the latest."

Tomorrow afternoon? Day *after* tomorrow? Cara felt her heart sink. Ian had dropped her off at the repair shop and gone on to meet Nick and Lucas over an hour ago, and it had taken that long to tow the car down from the mountain and get an estimate. She'd spent the past twenty minutes arguing with the airport car rental company over the lemon they'd rented her. They'd offered her another car, but because she was out of the area, they couldn't get it to her for at least two days. The best they could do was to let the auto shop in Wolf River make the repairs, and they'd pick up the bill.

How big of them. Either way, she was without transportation.

Looks like you're stuck with me, Shawnessy, whether you like it or not. She couldn't decide whether to smile or scream.

With a sigh she signed the estimate, then took the copy that Walt handed her. "Is the post office close by, and a place where I can get something to eat?"

"Post office is at the end of this block, and Papa Pete's is right around the corner. They make the best burgers and fries this side of the Mississippi." Walt gave her a toothy grin. "Tell Madge that Walt sent you and she'll throw in a chocolate shake for free. She's sweet on me."

The post office was closed for lunch, with a little paper clock on the locked door that gave the time the clerk would return. Cara could only imagine what the customers would do if a post office closed during lunch in Philadelphia. There'd probably be a riot, she thought with a smile, and found herself warming up to the slower pace and charm of small-town living. Not that she could live here, of course. She liked the hustle and bustle of a big city. But the change of pace from Philadelphia was refreshing, and while she was here, she intended to enjoy it.

She could already smell the delicious aroma of hamburgers grilling before she opened the glass door to Papa Pete's Down Home Diner. The restaurant was fifties decor—all original—with shiny maroon vinyl booths, chrome and Formica countertops, and alternating black and white floor tiles. The room was packed with a lunch crowd, and when she stepped inside, Cara suddenly understood what a bug felt like under a microscope. A stranger in a smalltown diner always drew attention, and she felt several pairs of eyes on her as a large woman with big platinum hair bustled toward her. Embroidered on her white uniform—the design also out of the fifties—was the name "Madge."

"You waiting for someone, sugar?" Madge's smile was friendly as she led Cara to a table.

Cara noticed a few heads turn in her direction as she slipped into a booth. "No, I'm alone."

The diner, noisy with conversation and busy bus boys only a moment ago, had grown strangely quiet. She felt like the person in that financial ad where everyone stopped to listen at the mention of a certain company.

Madge laid a plastic-coated menu on the table. "Aren't you the gal renting the cabin up at the lake? You were in town a few days ago, at the minimarket. Tracy told me you were right keen on apricots. Said your name was Carol."

There were limits to small-town charm, Cara thought, and decided she was going to have to be cautious of her purchases in town if she didn't want to be the center of attention.

Too late, she realized. Everyone in the diner was already staring or listening.

What the heck. The youngest of five, and the only girl, was used to being the center of attention.

"Not Carol." She smiled at the waitress. "Cara. Cara Sinclair. And you must be Madge. Walt at the repair shop said I should order a hamburger, that yours are the best."

"He likes her buns, too," a blond waitress called out from the counter, and several patrons laughed.

"Watch your mouth, Dixie," Madge called back, but it was all in fun. "The boy's a little sweet on me, that's all."

"We're all a little sweet on you, Madge, you know that." A young man wearing a cowboy hat winked at Madge, then tipped his hat to Cara. "How do, ma'am. Luke Sanders."

There was a sparkle in Madge's big brown eyes as she shook her head. "Watch out for these cowboys, sugar. Can't trust 'em as far as you can throw 'em."

"You threw Dutch Johnson clean into Mesa County last time he sassed you," a tall, lanky man called out from his bar stool at the counter.

Madge propped a hefty arm on one thick hip and glared at the man. "You're gonna be next, Leroy, if you don't mind your own business. And you're so skinny I could probably pitch you all the way to San Antonio."

Cara watched in awe as several customers, men and women, joined in to taunt Madge and Leroy. Mock insults flew like missiles, and within seconds the entire place had erupted into laughter. Just like dinner at her house when she was growing up, Cara thought with a smile. Or on those rare occasions when she and all her brothers managed to be in the same place at the same time. She hadn't realized until this minute just how long it had been, and how much she missed them.

She finished ordering her lunch between salvos and somehow felt as though she'd been initiated into the town by participating in the diner's free-for-all. Madge finally stomped off, supposedly to get a frying pan to bean Luke, the cowboy, for starting the whole thing. After a few more verbal attacks, the diner settled down.

That's when the questions started.

What'd you say your name was, honey?

Where you from?

You really come all the way from Philadelphia just to stay at the lake?

Before she knew it, a married couple had slid into the booth with her, and two ranch hands had pulled up chairs alongside. Everyone else was either listening or adding to the conversation whenever they could get a word in.

That's how Ian found her when he came into the diner.

Surrounded by townspeople, people he knew, people he'd grown up with, worked with. His eyes narrowed at the two ranch hands glued to Cara's side: Biff Hornsby and Luke Sanders. There were also a few he'd caroused with, he thought with a frown, remembering the two men.

Blast that tailor for taking so long with the fitting. It was bad enough being stuffed into a monkey suit and chalked up like a baseball field, but he'd also had to endure Lucas's and Nick's incessant questions about Cara.

He made his way to the table, caught the tail end of a story Cara was telling about a bigamist she'd tracked down while she was working for an insurance company in Philadelphia. What the two wives had done to their unfaithful husband when they found him made the men wince and the women clap with appreciation.

Shaking his head, he struggled to hold back a grin. He should have known better than to leave her on her own. A woman like Cara was bound to draw attention, not only because of her looks and because she was a stranger in town, but there was something else about her, something…engaging, was his first thought. She made a room come alive just by walking into it.

Something shifted in his chest when he heard her laugh. Something he couldn't quite identify. Something he was certain he didn't like at all.

"Why, look, Tom, it's Ian Shawnessy!" Joan Buford, who was sitting in the booth across from Cara, grabbed her husband's arm. "Beverly Patterson told us you were back in town and staying up at the lake. I declare, Ian, you must have grown another four inches since I saw you last."

Ian smiled at the brunette who'd been fresh out of college when she'd been his seventh-grade math teacher, noticed there were streaks of gray at her temples now. No doubt, he and Lucas and Nick had put a few of those there when she'd had them all in the same class almost twenty years ago. It was a miracle she'd survived that first year.

"Nice to see you, Mrs. Buford. Mr. Buford."

"Why, Cara here is staying at the lake, too." Joan gestured toward Cara. "Have you two met?"

"I was fishing when we bumped into each other down by the lake a few days ago." Ian turned his smile on Cara. "Caught me a big one that day."

"Men and their fish stories." Cara rolled her eyes, which brought a round of laughter. "Everyone knows it doesn't count if the fish gets away."

"We'll meet up again," Ian said with confidence. "Next time that fish won't be so lucky."

"I'm sure luck had nothing to do with it." Cara smiled sweetly. "But if you do meet up again, my money's on the fish."

"Killian Shawnessy!" Madge slid Cara's order, complete with a chocolate shake, on the table. "'Bout time you showed up here. I was starting to take your absence from my place as a personal affront. Come here and give this old broad a hug."

The Army could have used this woman for a secret weapon, Ian thought, as the woman wrapped her bulky arms around him and squeezed. Air rushed out of his lungs.

"Let the boy go," Leroy hollered out from the counter. "He's turning blue."

"I'll show you blue." Madge released Ian and shook a fist at her heckler. "Black-and-blue all over that fence post you call a body. Okay, everyone, show's over." She shooed the crowd away from the table. "Back to your own seats."

Madge tweaked Ian's cheek. "Double cheeseburger, medium rare, mayo and lettuce, no onion, chili fries and chocolate mint shake."

Ian shook his head in amazement as the woman headed back toward the kitchen. In Washington, when he wasn't traveling, he ate at the same coffee shop at least four times a week and the waitress couldn't remember if he even took cream with his coffee, let alone if he wanted an onion on his burger. He hadn't seen Madge in over fourteen years, and she remembered, in detail, everything he used to order.

Cara was staring at him in wonder as he slid into the seat opposite her. "That woman hugged you and tweaked your cheek. And you actually let her."

"Nobody argues with Madge." Ian reached for a French fry and popped it into his mouth. "Not if they want to live or ever eat one of her hamburgers again. Why didn't you wait at the repair shop for me?"

"Those happen to be my fries," she said dryly when Ian reached for a bottle of ketchup. "And why would I wait for you?"

"You're going to need a ride back to your cabin, aren't

you? Unless your bags are in the Jeep and you've decided to go back to Philadelphia?''

"'Fraid not, Shawnessy. Not until you agree to go with me." She reached for her hamburger and sank her teeth in. "Besides," she said around a soft moan, "now I have another good reason to stay here. Walt's right—this is the best burger I ever had."

"Wait till you try the shake." He reached for her glass. "I've dreamed about one of these for fourteen years." He took a big swig of the thick chocolate drink, then sighed with pleasure. "Now *that* was worth waiting for."

Laughing, she tried the milkshake, then closed her eyes on a groan. He was right. It was good. Better than good, in fact.

The din of the restaurant surrounded them; people laughing and talking, Madge shouting orders, the clanking of silverware and plates. But it was all background, and Cara felt as if she and Ian were alone. Just two people enjoying a meal and each other's company.

She took another sip of the milkshake, then scooted it back to him. "Why did you wait so long to come back, Shawnessy? You must have missed your friends here, not to mention these burgers and shakes."

He took another deep swig of the frozen drink, then shrugged and settled back in the booth. "I was never close to anyone other than Nick and Lucas. We all scattered after high school. Nick was traveling and racing and Lucas was busy building Blackhawk Enterprises."

"And you started your company," she said. "What made you decide to manufacture cellular phones?"

He glanced away, but not before she caught something in his eyes, a hesitation of some kind. She thought it strange, since most men never stopped talking about their jobs or business. But then, she'd already discovered that Ian wasn't most men.

"It just sort of happened," he finally said. "It's a living."

"A job should be more than just a living," she said firmly. "You should love it, be passionate about it. It's like a marriage."

He lifted a brow. "What do you know about marriage? Have you been there?"

"Not yet. But I will, when it feels right." She took another bite of her burger and chewed thoughtfully. "What about you? Hasn't the hearth-and-home bug ever bit you, Flash?"

"I lived in four different foster homes from the time I was nine." He took another swig of her milkshake. "I got enough hearth and home to last me a lifetime, Blondie."

There was something in his voice she couldn't read, something in his eyes. "Were they that bad?" she asked quietly.

He shook his head. "They were fine. A bed to sleep in, food on the table. Everything I needed."

Not nearly, she thought. Not even close. He just didn't know there was more than that. He'd never had a chance. But he had one now, with Margaret.

"Ian, come to Philadelphia with me. Meet your grandmother. Please, just give her a chance."

"You don't give up, do you?"

She shook her head. "Never."

He sighed, then did something that shocked her. He smiled. Not one of his sarcastic, mocking smiles, but a genuine, eye-crinkling smile that made her stomach twist into several knots.

The impact of his smile caught her so completely off guard she went still. Her heart pounded, a slow, heavy thud in her chest. When his gaze dropped to her mouth, a warmth spread through her that seeped all the way to her toes.

"I'm *not* going to Philadelphia with you, Blondie."

Shaking off the powerful need humming through her blood, Cara leaned forward. "Twenty says you will, Flash."

He lifted both brows, then reached into his pocket and pulled out his wallet. "I'll show you mine, if you show me yours. On the table."

She pulled a twenty out of her purse and slid it to the middle of the table. When Madge showed up with Ian's food, Cara handed the waitress the two bills.

"Ian and I have a little bet going, Madge. Think you could hold this for a few days?"

"Sure thing, sugar." The money disappeared down the woman's large cleavage. "This have anything to do with that fish you were arguing about earlier?"

Cara grinned at Ian, was surprised when he grinned back. "Something like that."

"You just let me know who wins the bet." Madge patted her bosom. "For now, it's safe as gold in Fort Knox."

After the waitress left, Ian reached for his hamburger. "The wedding is Saturday," he said around a big bite. "I'm leaving on Sunday. You haven't got much time."

"I've got all the time I need and then some." The man was much too smug for his own good, Cara thought, and she couldn't wait to be the one to knock him down a few pegs. "Oh, that reminds me, do you mind if we stop by the post office after lunch? There's a package from Margaret waiting for you."

Six

He couldn't sleep.

At midnight he tossed the covers off and punched his pillow. At twelve-thirty, he stared at the sliver of light coming through his bedroom window and counted backward from fifty. At one o'clock, he swore and sat on the edge of the bed.

He wasn't going to open the damn package.

Cara had left it on the front seat of the truck's cab when he'd dropped her off at her cabin. She'd looked so pleased with herself when she'd hopped out of the truck and waved goodbye. The woman was enough to drive any man crazy.

He thought about her lying in bed right now, that long, curvy body, her soft, silky skin. He imagined the feel of her breasts against his chest as he covered her body with his and pressed her into the mattress.

His fists tightened on the rumpled sheets. Frustrated, he

decided he was better off thinking about the package than Cara Sinclair.

What could possibly be inside the shoebox-size parcel that would matter to him? Some pictures of people he'd never known? A few mementos that had belonged to a father who had died before he was even born? Or maybe a present, a bribe of some kind to entice him to come to Philadelphia.

He didn't care if the Queen's jewels were in that box. He wasn't going anywhere but back to Washington. His leave was up in six days, and he'd already been assigned to an undercover unit in Cairo. He'd be on a plane a few days from now, then gone for at least three months.

With a sigh he dragged both hands over his scalp. It was his third high-risk assignment in eighteen months. The cell phone company had been his front for the past ten years, since he'd been recruited into the Agency straight from the Marines. As far as everyone in the outside world knew, he was a simple business man traveling overseas.

Strange how ten years could feel like a lifetime.

He wasn't sure why he did it anymore. Not for the money. He'd never cared about money, and besides, he'd invested well over the past ten years and didn't have to work another day if he didn't want to. And he certainly didn't do it for the rush. The first few years he'd thrived on the adrenaline, the danger, but that honeymoon was long over, too.

Yanking on his jeans, he stumbled to the kitchen and turned on the light. He thought about a beer, but knew that wouldn't be strong enough to cut the edge off the tension knotting his body. There was a bottle of Johnny Walker in the cupboard. He'd been saving it for the prewedding dinner at Lucas and Julianna's house tomorrow night—tonight, he corrected himself.

Oh, what the hell.

He pulled the bottle out of the cupboard, grabbed a glass, then sat at the kitchen table.

And stared at the package sitting ten inches away from him.

It was harmless in appearance. Brown paper and shiny packing tape; Ian doubted it weighed more than one pound. The return address was handwritten in black pen. The writing was as feminine as it was formal and neat: "Margaret Muldoon. West Third Street. Philadelphia, Pennsylvania."

He broke the whisky label and poured himself a shot.

Outside, an owl hooted in the darkness. Inside, the clock over the stove ticked the seconds away.

Dammit to hell.

He snatched up the package, ripped off the paper, then opened the cardboard box.

It was filled with envelopes. Different sizes, different colors. The top envelope, yellowed with age, had the number one on it. The card inside was pale green, with a white kitten and black spotted puppy. "For Baby's First Birthday," it read.

A child's birthday card?

He opened the card, read the generic greeting-card poem inside, then the handwritten inscription. "For my grandbaby, where ever you might be. My love goes with you always. Grandmama."

Ian quickly glanced through the stack of envelopes. All of them were birthday cards. There were thirty-three.

He was thirty-three.

Bewildered, he stared at the box.

His grandmother, a woman he'd never met, who hadn't even known if he was dead or alive, had bought him a birthday card every year for thirty-three years?

He downed the shot of whisky, then reached for the second card. There were circus clowns and animals hanging from a large number two. The handwritten note inside the card read, "You must be so big by now, and talking, too. I wonder often if you are a boy or a girl, if you have your father's eyes, your mother's hair. If you know you have a grandmama who loves you very much."

He stared at the words, disbelieving. These were *his* birthday cards, each one of them meant for *him*.

The notes inside became longer with each consecutive card. Year five she asked about kindergarten, year seven she wondered about sports and music. Each year asked different questions about school or likes and dislikes, all of them were signed: "With love from Grandmama."

Ian smiled at number twelve. There was a photograph of a grinning orangutan on the front of the card, its big hairy hand holding a dozen brightly colored balloons. Inside, under the simple "Happy Birthday" wish, Margaret wrote, "How grown-up you must be. A handsome young man, or a stunning young woman. I miss sharing these years with you, but you are in my heart always. I can only pray that one day God will smile on me and bring us together."

Confused, he stared at the stack of cards piled on the table and rubbed at the tightness inside his bare chest. He didn't understand why Margaret had done this, or why she had continued year after year, when the hope of ever finding a grandchild—a child that might not even exist—had proven so futile. If nothing else, Margaret Muldoon was tenacious.

He downed the lump in his throat with another shot of whisky, and unbidden, the thought of another woman, equally tenacious, came to mind. One considerably younger, one that had him in chaos since the first moment he'd laid eyes on her.

Cara, with her smiling green eyes and sassy mouth. He

remembered the kiss he'd given her that first day, a simple kiss meant only to keep her quiet. But there'd been nothing simple about it at all. Even now he could feel the soft press of her lips under his, he could still taste the sweetness of apricots.

Dammit, anyway!

He sent the cards flying with a sweep of his arm. She'd brought all this aggravation into his life. Aggravation he didn't need, and sure as hell didn't want. No woman had given him sleepless nights before or intruded endlessly into his thoughts. No woman had ever left him wanting or tied him up in knots so tightly he couldn't think straight.

He jumped, then swore when the phone in the living room rang. It had to be Jordan. No doubt she was more than annoyed with him for not calling her, and the fact that it was almost two in the morning wouldn't matter even remotely to her.

He grabbed the phone on the third ring. "Dammit, Jordan, get off my back. I'll call you when I'm good and ready."

"It's not Jordan," a feminine voice whispered. "It's Cara."

"Cara?" His hand tightened on the phone. "What's wrong?"

"Ah, if you aren't too busy, could you come over here?" There was a sharp intake of breath. "I think there's someone trying to break in the front door."

Cara stood behind the door in the pitch-darkness, a cast-iron skillet in her hands. The scratching sound she'd heard only a moment ago had stopped. Except for the pounding of her heart, now there was only silence.

Breath held, shivering in her thin cotton tank top and boxers, she waited.

The doorknob creaked, then turned.

Her hands tightened around the handle of the heavy frying pan; she sucked in a breath as the door slowly opened. When the dark shape stepped into the room, she raised the pan over her head.

"Cara?"

Ian? Too late to stop her swing, she brought the pan down, though not as hard as she would have. It landed with a solid hit, and she heard a hard object scoot across the wood floor. An explicit string of swear words filled the quiet.

"Oh, my God, Ian!" The frying pan slipped from her hands and clattered to the floor. "Are you all right?"

"Sure I am," he muttered irritably. "You just cracked my skull in half, why wouldn't I be?"

"How did you get here so fast? I just called you." She reached out into the darkness, made contact with his head. "I thought you were a prowler."

"Ow!" He jerked away. "What the hell did you hit me with, a slab of concrete?"

"Frying pan." She closed the door, then took his hand and carefully dragged him to the living room sofa. "I think I broke it."

"My head or the frying pan?" he grumbled, but let himself be pulled down on the sofa beside her. "Where the hell is my gun?"

She flipped on the lamp beside the couch. Soft light spilled over them. "You brought a *gun?*"

"No, I was wondering where my gun at home is." He dropped his head into his hands. "Of course I brought a gun. You said someone was breaking in."

"I just didn't realize you had one, that's all." She spotted the pistol on the floor by the coffee table and shivered at the sight of it. She hated guns. "Is it loaded?"

He turned his head sideways, glanced at her with a look that told her it definitely was. She shivered again.

When his eyes closed in pain again, she reached for him. "Here, let me look at your head."

"You've done enough for one night." He jerked away when she touched his head.

She frowned at him. "Stop acting like a baby and come here."

"Baby? Me? You're the one who called me, remember?"

"I heard something."

"And you were scared."

"I wasn't scared," she lied. "I had the situation completely under control. I only called you in case I needed backup."

"You were scared." He brought his face close to hers and narrowed his eyes. "Admit it, Sinclair."

She sighed with exasperation. Admitting weakness to this man was like riding a motorcycle without a helmet. Sooner or later she was going to be sorry.

More than likely it was going to be sooner.

"All right, maybe I was scared, just a little bit," she admitted. "It could have been a bear out there, or a patient escaped from a mental institution."

"At least that would be someone you could identify with," he said testily, then yelped when she yanked on his ears and pulled his head onto her lap. "Hey, that hurt."

"Be still and keep quiet."

He closed his eyes on a grimace, tolerating her ministrations. The light from the lamp hardened his features, sharpened his tightly held jaw and firm mouth. Cara thought he had the fierce look of an outlaw being led to the gallows.

"How *did* you get here so fast, anyway? Oh, that's right," she said sweetly. "I forgot they called you Flash. I hope that doesn't extend into all areas of your life, Shaw-nessy.''

He gave a low growl as he started to sit, but she cupped his face in her hands and forced him to be still. A coarse, day's growth of beard rasped against her palms and sent currents of electricity up her arms. She felt disgusted with herself. She'd wounded the man, now she wanted to jump his bones.

Maybe he was right. Maybe she did belong in a mental institution. Sighing heavily, she touched her fingers to his temple. ''Now lie still and let me look.''

And she did, though not at his head. Her gaze dropped to his bare chest, and though it was hardly the time, it was impossible not to admire his physique, the strong masculine angles of solid muscle, sprinkled with dark, coarse hair. Her hands itched to slide over that broad expanse of sinew and feel the touch of his skin under her fingertips. Her attention dropped lower, to his flat, hard stomach, then lower still, to the unsnapped top of his jeans. Heat flooded through her, and she jerked her gaze away, thankful that Ian's eyes were still tightly closed.

The back of his head was nestled across her thighs, his cheek and ear pressed against her stomach. Soft ribbons of heat curled from her waist downward. She willed her hands not to tremble as she lightly skimmed her fingers through his thick hair and over his scalp.

He sucked in a breath when she touched a rising knot on top of his head. ''Oops.''

He frowned. ''What, oops?''

''Well, the good news is, there's no blood. The bad news is, you'll have a bump the size of a Volkswagen.''

''Gosh, I'm so glad you gave me the good news first,'' he mumbled, but the edge of anger that had been in his voice a moment ago was gone now. She felt the tension in his shoulders ease as he relaxed his head on her legs.

Cara knew she should move away. They were both half-naked, lying on the couch with the darkness surrounding them. She in her tank top and boxers, Ian wearing only a pair of jeans. Her fingers moved restlessly through his hair, though they both knew she'd already found the damage she'd inflicted.

And still she couldn't stop herself.

Nor did he stop her.

Her fingernails lightly scraped over his scalp, and he relaxed under her touch. She was certain he could hear the heavy beat of her heart.

"Did you see anyone outside?" she asked quietly. "Or anything?"

He shook his head, inadvertently rubbing against her belly. She had to remind herself to breathe.

He still hadn't opened his eyes, and she took advantage of the opportunity to explore his face. She discovered a small, jagged scar over his left eye and a long, razor-thin scar under his chin. A dark shadow of a beard covered his strong, square jaw. Transfixed, she stared at his mouth, and just the thought of running her fingers over those firm lips made her hand tingle.

This was dangerous, she knew. As dangerous as it was foolish. She should get up, or at least move away.

She didn't.

"Something was out there." She did her best to focus on what had frightened her, instead of the sensations washing through her body at the moment. "Or someone. I didn't imagine it."

"Well, whoever or whatever it was, is gone now. Unlike the bump on my head," he reminded her.

"I'll get some ice."

She started to rise, but he reached up and circled her wrists with his hands.

"No."

It was not a request, but a command. He opened his eyes and stared at her. She couldn't breath. Couldn't think.

The intensity of his dark gaze excited, yet terrified her at the same time. Her previous fear suddenly seemed like nothing compared to what she was experiencing now. She tried to speak, to laugh this craziness off, but her throat felt like cotton. The tension between them felt like a living, breathing creature, an animal coiled and ready to spring from the darkness.

She was hardly a woman of the world when it came to sex, but she wasn't a virgin, either, in spite of her brothers' determination that she remain celibate her entire life. They'd been successful deterring her suitors until she'd escaped to college, and by that time she'd been much too curious to delay the experience. She'd chosen her first lover carefully, but with her head instead of her heart, and the relationship was doomed from the start. Not wanting a repeat of that situation, she'd decided not to settle, and had waited for the fireworks she'd heard so much about. And waited and waited.

And now here she was, a regular Fourth-of-July explosion going on inside her, and it was all wrong. *He* was all wrong.

He brought her hands to his mouth, pressed feather-soft kisses on each palm. Her heart slammed in her chest.

"Ian," she gasped as his tongue caressed her wrists. "I don't think this is such a good idea."

"It's not."

He brought her hands to his chest, then slipped his arms around her waist as he turned his head into her stomach and pressed his mouth to her navel. Her head dropped back on a soft moan. Thin cotton was the only thing separating his mouth from her bare skin, and it was all she could do to stop herself from ripping the tank top off.

He took his time nuzzling her. The heat of his mouth and breath stoked the fire building inside her. Her fingers curled over his neck and upper shoulders; his skin was damp, the scent woodsy, masculine. She heard the sound of her own labored breathing, then the low groan from deep in his throat as he pulled her closer to him.

She'd never experienced anything like this before; passion that consumed so completely, so thoroughly. She hadn't known it even existed beyond the movies and books. Sex had been pleasant enough, but never earth-shattering, never overpowering.

Never devastating.

That thought flew apart when he used his teeth to push the unwanted fabric out of his way and bared her stomach to him. His mouth was hot on her skin; he nipped and tasted the soft flesh as he slowly moved upward. She felt herself melt under his touch, her bones soften like warm taffy.

His hands slid under soft cotton and cupped her breasts. She arched upward on a gasp when his thumbs caressed her hardened nipples. Sensations, as exquisite as they were intense, rippled through her. She burrowed her fingers into his scalp, wanting more of this incredible pleasure.

He gave it to her. His mouth replaced his thumb, and she caught her breath on a soft, low moan. His wet, hot tongue swirled over the sensitive peak, sending hot currents of pain-pleasure through her.

She had to touch him, it was absolutely necessary. Her hands roamed over the solid muscles of his upper arms, slid over his wide, strong shoulders. He felt like a raging river of liquid steel under her, and she let herself be swept up in the current of passion engulfing them both.

"Ian." His name was a soft, breathless whisper on her lips. "Ian, oh, my—" Her words were cut off as he moved to her other breast and offered the same delicious attention with his mouth and tongue.

It felt as if she were on fire; flames licked at her skin. She needed him closer. Impatient, she cupped his head in her hands, then dragged her fingers over his scalp.

He sucked in a sharp breath and swore, then slowly sat as he dropped his head into his hands.

In her dazed state, it took a moment to realize why he'd moved away from her, then she groaned and dropped her head back against the sofa. His head. She'd completely forgotten she'd bashed in his head with a frying pan. Of course he'd be in pain. And she'd just dug her fingernails directly into the source of that pain.

Embarrassment flamed on her cheeks. Not only because she'd hurt him, but because of what had just happened between them—not to mention what would have happened. She quickly pulled her tank top back into place.

"Oh, Ian, I'm so sorry. I...I wasn't thinking."

Still holding his head in his hands, he let out a long, slow breath. "That makes two of us."

"I'll get some ice."

She started to rise, but once again he snagged her hand and pulled her back down. "Cara," he said quietly. "I opened the package."

The package? *The package.* She hadn't thought of it once since she'd smashed him over the head. Her body was still humming from his kisses, and she was finding it hard to think about the package even now that he'd reminded her. Especially with his hand still touching her arm and his thigh pressed against hers.

She had to dig deep, but she mustered up a light tone. "So you caved, did you? How long did you hold out?"

He chuckled at that, then winced from the effort. "Do you know what was inside?"

"Margaret didn't tell me." She wanted to brush the hair off his forehead and kiss his temple. Instead, she tugged at the edge of her cotton knit boxers, wishing she'd worn sweats or flannel pajamas. Anything that would have covered her, that would have made her feel less vulnerable.

"They were birthday cards."

"Birthday cards?"

"She'd bought one for me, every year, from my first birthday on, and kept them all."

Cara frowned. "But she didn't know about you, if you even existed."

"She didn't know my name," he said with a sigh, "or even if I was a boy or girl, but she believed that I—her grandchild—was alive."

The thought made Cara's eyes tear. All these years, even though there'd never been one shred of evidence to prove that her grandchild had lived after birth, Margaret had clung to her hope, to what she believed in her heart. Every card was a symbol of that hope. And of her love.

"Ian—" she scooted to the edge of the couch and turned to face him "—you're Margaret's only grandchild. Don't you see how important you are to her, how much she needs to see you, if only once before she dies?"

He shook his head slowly. "If I go, she'll just want to see me one more time after that. Then it will be Thanksgiving and Christmas, long, chatty phone calls every Sunday. Vacations. I can't give her any of that, Cara. If I go even once, I'll only end up hurting her more."

It was the first time he'd acted like he gave a damn at all. If only a little, maybe that whack on the head had softened him, she thought with a smile. She knew he wasn't going to like her observations on the subject one little bit, but that hadn't stopped her before, and it wouldn't stop her now.

"It scares you, doesn't it?"

Eyes narrowed, he glanced over at her. "What the hell are you talking about?"

"You're afraid that it isn't just Margaret who might want a relationship," she said evenly. "You're afraid you might want one with her, too."

His laugh was dry. "You're crazy."

"You're safe where you are right now," she went on, even though she saw his expression darkening. "No serious commitment or responsibility, just a couple of old chums you get together with now and then. But a grandmother, that's an entirely different story. You might care about her, worry about her, maybe even love her. She might matter to you. And that, Killian Shawnessy Muldoon, absolutely terrifies you."

A muscle worked at his jaw. "Was this some kind of a setup, Blondie? Call me over here in the middle of the night, then get me in your bed so I'll agree to go to Philadelphia? Some girls will do anything for twenty bucks."

His crude verbal blow struck her square in her chest, sucked the air from her lungs. Her impulse was to slap him, but then he'd know how deeply he'd hurt her, and she refused to show him weakness.

She drew in a slow, deep breath and stood. "I apologize for calling you, and for hitting you. What happened between us after that was unprofessional of me, and I assure you it won't happen again."

He scrubbed a hand over his face. "Cara, look, I—"

"I'd appreciate it if you'd leave." She moved toward the front door and opened it. "Now."

He rose stiffly from the couch, picked up his gun off the floor and moved toward her. When he paused at the front door, she lifted her chin and met his heavy gaze, dared him to speak, to say just one thing. This time she wouldn't hold back, and she sure as hell wouldn't apologize.

His eyes went black with a mixture of anger and frustration, then he clamped his lips tightly together and stormed out the door.

It took tremendous restraint on her part not to slam the door after him. She closed it quietly, then leaned back against the cold wood and fought the threatening tears. He wasn't worth it, she told herself over and over. He wasn't.

He wasn't.

She looked down at the doorknob and frowned. Ian had just walked in, but she was certain she'd locked the door before she went to bed.

Hadn't she?

She didn't know what she was doing these past couple of days. It was easy to forget things when her mind was so preoccupied with Ian. And now, after what had just happened between them, she'd be lucky if she remembered how to tie her shoes.

With a sigh she locked the door and headed back to her bed, but she had the distinct feeling she wouldn't be getting much sleep.

Seven

Ian was certain that a tiny little man with a great big hammer was trying to get out of his skull. The pounding centered in his temples and radiated upward to the top of his throbbing head. He attempted to move, and the pain shot through his brain like a red-hot pinball racking up championship points.

Very, very carefully, he opened his eyes, then slammed them shut again when he felt the burn of sunlight on his eyeballs. He imagined that vampires went through the same agony when their skin met daylight.

He reached for his pillow, but found empty air instead.

Confused, he shifted his weight from his back to his side, then gave a strangled yelp as he fell face first onto the floor. With a groan he opened his eyes again, blinked several times until the room came into focus.

What the hell was he doing on the sofa in the living room? Well, actually, he was now on the *floor,* if a person wanted to get technical. He just couldn't quite remember *how* he happened to be here.

Closing his eyes, he laid his cheek on the cool hardwood and drew in several slow breaths. When the pain in his head began to ease, he rolled to his back and carefully opened his eyes to stare up at the open-beam pine ceiling.

On a groan he closed his eyes again.

And remembered.

Damn.

Cara's phone call, her bashing his head in. Her fingers sliding over his scalp, the feel of her soft, silky skin under his hands and mouth...

Oh, yes, he remembered, all right. In detail. He'd downed half a bottle of whisky after that, trying to wash the sweet taste of her out of his system. The need and the longing. It hadn't worked, of course. And now he had to pay the consequences of his stupidity. Stupidity that went much farther than a cotton-dry mouth and pounding skull.

Some girls will do anything for twenty bucks.

Swearing, he sat slowly, brought his legs up and rested his pulsating head on his knees. What had possessed him to say something so completely out of line? He knew she hadn't pretended someone was breaking into her cabin just to get him over there. She might have lied to him the first time he'd laid eyes on her, when he'd caught her watching him from across the lake, but she'd been honest since then. She wasn't the kind of woman who played coy games of seduction, and even as much as she wanted him to come to Philadelphia, he didn't believe for a second she'd go to bed with him as a means of persuasion.

So why had he said it?

He could still see the slash of hurt and shock on her face when he'd accused her of lying. She'd recovered quickly, her face expressionless as she'd stared him square in the eye and asked him to leave. He wished she'd yelled at him, cried, hit him with that frying pan again—anything but given him that cold, empty stare.

Well, fine then, he thought irritably, lifting his head and testing the extent of the damage he'd done to himself. Maybe he'd be rid of her now. Maybe she'd stop bothering him about going to Philadelphia to meet Margaret. He was sure she was a nice old lady, but he wasn't going. Nothing, and no one, was going to change that.

When the phone rang from the end table beside the sofa, he covered his ears and moaned. He wasn't going to answer it. He didn't want to talk to Jordan, she'd only increase the throbbing in his head with one of her tirades. It might be Nick, though, calling to remind him about dinner tonight at Lucas and Julianna's house, but Ian decided he definitely needed some aspirin before talking to Nick.

But what if it was someone else, someone with fiery green eyes and silky blond hair....

He had to crawl to the phone, which seemed fitting if it was Cara. He picked it up on the fourth ring.

"Yeah," he mumbled, because that was all he could manage given the dust-dry state of his mouth.

"That you, Ian?"

"Walt?" The mechanic's drawl was unmistakable.

"The one and only. You still sleeping at eleven o'clock, son?"

He hadn't realized how late it was. "You call for a reason, or just to see what my sleeping habits are?"

Walt's chuckle was deep and gravelly. "Well, I tried calling Miss Sinclair first, but couldn't get an answer. I thought it might be important, so seein's how you're friends and all—"

"Walt," Ian said with a sigh, "could you please get to the point?"

"Well, son, it's like this..."

Ian's eyes narrowed tightly as he listened. When he hung up, he uttered one seemingly appropriate word, then headed straight for the bedroom to get dressed.

He had to find Cara. Now.

Cara sat on the soft, leaf-covered ground and leaned back against a tree stump. The cabin walls had closed in on her, and without a car, her only other escape was the forest.

With a sigh she closed her eyes and rested her head back against the tree stump. The late-morning air was warm, but not unbearable as it had been earlier in the week. The scent of dried leaves and pine surrounded her, carried on the soft breeze that lifted the ends of her hair.

She'd thought about giving up. Maybe asking the honeymoon couple or the father and son to give her a lift into town where she could wait until her car was repaired, then drive to the airport and take the first plane out. Lord knew it would be easier than dealing with Ian. But then, *walking* back to Philadelphia would be easier than dealing with Ian.

But Cara knew she couldn't leave, any more than she could give up. Margaret was too important to her. Cara had told her friend that she'd bring her grandson home, and she wouldn't leave until every last card was played.

She'd hit a button with him last night. She'd gotten too close to the truth when she'd told him he was afraid he might come to care for Margaret. That's why he'd lashed out at her as he had. A man like Killian Shawnessy took pride in his independence and I-hunt-alone attitude. The birthday cards that Margaret had sent put a chink in his armor, and he didn't like it one little bit. It took a lot of the sting out of the insult he'd tossed at her, but she'd be lying to say it didn't still hurt.

She'd never been one to hold grudges or stay angry, but

in Ian's case, Cara decided she would make an exception.
She'd like nothing better than to shove him over a cliff.
But maybe just a short one, instead of the deep canyon
she'd visualized last night.

And it made her all the more angry that even after what
he'd said to her, she still wanted his mouth on her mouth,
still wanted his hands on her body.

Damn you, Killian Shawnessy.

"There you are."

Her eyes flew open at the deep sound of his voice so
close to her. The man was quiet as a mouse—no, make that
a snake, she amended. And how had he found her, anyway?

She felt a small amount of satisfaction that he looked
ragged around the edges. His hair hadn't been combed, his
jeans and red flannel shirt were wrinkled, his eyes were
bloodshot, and he hadn't shaved.

And he still looked sexy as hell, blast it.

But strangely enough, he also looked angry.

"Where have you been?"

She blinked. "Excuse me?"

"It was a simple question." Jamming his hands on his
hips, he marched toward her. "Where have you been?"

Obviously in the *Twilight Zone,* she thought in amazement. What else could explain his bizarre behavior? "I fail
to see how where I am or where I've been is any business
of yours."

"You've been gone for hours." Frowning, he stood over
her. "People get lost up here if they don't stay on the paths.
They didn't find one guy named Wallace Walker for six
months. All that was left of him were bones and a pair of
sunglasses."

"Interesting image." If he was trying to scare her, it was
working. "And how would you know I've been gone for
hours?"

"Walt's been trying to reach you. Look, Cara, we need to talk." He held out a hand to help her up. "Let's go back to the cabin."

She ignored his hand. "Why has Walt been trying to reach me? Is my car ready? Oh, no." She closed her eyes and moaned. "Please don't tell me it's not ready. It's not, is it? Damn! I can't—"

"Cara—"

"—be without a car—"

"Cara—"

"—until next week, I've got to-

"Cara!"

He wrapped his hands around her shoulders and lifted her to her feet. Startled into silence, she stared at him. "What?"

"Somebody messed with your car."

"Messed with my car? You mean it was vandalized at Walt's shop?"

"Before you had it towed to Walt's. He found evidence that your rear brakes were tampered with. That's why they failed."

It took a long moment for his words to sink in, and still she didn't understand. Maybe she *had* hit him over the head too hard last night. She frowned, then laughed. "That's ridiculous."

"No more ridiculous than someone trying to break into your cabin last night."

"You don't know that." Now he was really stretching it. "That could have been an animal."

He let go of her arms, then reached into his shirt pocket and pulled out a safety pin. "I found this on your porch this morning."

She looked at the safety pin, then cocked an eyebrow at

him. "And your point is what? That all burglars are prepared for emergency clothing repairs?"

"The end is sanded smooth, which makes it a tool for
picking locks." He slipped it back into his pocket. "I also
found fresh bootprints that didn't belong to you or me."

The breeze picked up, scattering leaves at their feet. A
slow chill slithered up her spine. "You're making this up
to scare me off."

He shook his head. "You can call Walt and ask him
yourself if you don't believe me."

She *didn't* believe this, not any of it. It was insane. But
she *had* locked her door last night, she was certain of it,
and it had been unlocked when Ian came in.

"What are you saying? That someone wants to hurt me?
I don't know anyone in Wolf River besides—" Her eyes
widened suddenly as she stared at him. She put a hand to
her throat, took a step backward.

"Oh, for heaven's sake, Sinclair—" he rolled his eyes
"—it isn't me."

She released the breath she'd been holding, felt silly that
she'd considered the possibility. "Well, you gotta admit. I
have made you pretty mad."

"Blondie, as far as I'm concerned," he said dryly, "you
haven't even come close to seeing mad, but you've definitely pushed the wrong button on someone."

She thought about the cliff her car had almost gone over,
the prowler at her cabin. That was one hell of a big button.
But it just wasn't possible. It couldn't be.

"I don't believe it." She shook her head. "This is Wolf
River. Why would anyone here go to such extremes to harm
me?"

"Maybe it isn't anyone from Wolf River." He stared at
her thoughtfully. "Didn't you tell me it was your job to
uncover insurance and company fraud? You said you were

good at it. I have to assume you have an inventory of unhappy victims.''

She did, of course, though the people she'd exposed didn't know who she was. But if someone found out—she felt her pulse skip at the thought—well, they wouldn't exactly be inviting her over for Thanksgiving dinner.

Still, it was just too far out-there.

''It doesn't make sense.'' She blew out a breath and dragged a hand through her hair. ''Why would someone go to the extra expense and trouble to follow me all the way up here? Why wouldn't they just go after me in Philadelphia?''

''Maybe because there'd be less of a connection,'' Ian suggested. ''Especially if you lost control of your car and ended up at the bottom of a canyon. It would just look like an accident.''

''Breaking into my cabin wouldn't look like an accident,'' she insisted. ''The authorities would know it was intentional.''

''You're leaving in two days. Maybe they're getting desperate and don't care. There'd be no witnesses, and if there were no clues, there'd be nothing to trace back.''

She couldn't believe she was standing here, analyzing how and why someone might kill her. When a twig broke in the brush behind them, she flew into Ian's arms. A squirrel ran out of the brush, sat up and twitched its tail at them before darting off again. She let out a long, slow breath.

Embarrassed at her skittishness, Cara forced a soft laugh and placed her palms on Ian's chest to push away.

He tugged her back.

She could feel the heat of his body through his clothes, it poured into her, seeped into her blood. Her knees felt weak, her skin felt hot and tight.

How could this be happening? One minute they were

discussing someone's plot to murder her, and in the blink of an eye, she was melting in his arms.

"Cara," he said her name softly.

"Hmm?" She stared at her hands on his chest. His flannel shirt felt soft under her fingers.

"I was out of line last night. I shouldn't have said what I said." He drew in a deep breath. "Maybe you were right, just a little. Maybe I don't like the idea of having the responsibility of a family."

Surprised not only at his apology, but at his admission she might be right, she looked up at him.

"Come to Philadelphia with me, Ian," she said quietly. "Just meet Margaret, that's all. No strings attached, no guilt if you decide not to see her again."

He shook his head slowly. "I can't go to Philadelphia."

"Can't or won't?"

"Both." He reached up and snagged a leaf from her hair, then softly stroked it over her jaw. She cursed the involuntary shudder that vibrated through her body.

"In the meantime," he said, "why don't I take you into town to talk to the sheriff?"

"Talk to the sheriff about what? That maybe someone tampered with my car and maybe someone tried to break into my cabin? What can they do?" She thought about all the paperwork, the wasted time. "I'm only here two more days, I can be careful. I'll go to the police when I get back home."

"If you live that long." He sighed heavily. "All right, then, get your bag packed."

"Didn't you hear me, Shawnessy? I'm not going anywhere. I refuse to be scared off, and I'm not giving up on you, either."

He hesitated at her words, then raised a brow. "But you are going somewhere, Blondie. You're moving in with me."

She'd argued, of course, but he won. She might be stubborn as a mule, Ian mused, but she wasn't stupid. If someone was after her, she'd be a sitting duck up in the mountains alone. Reluctantly, she'd finally given in and moved her things over to his place.

He still couldn't believe he had even considered moving her in with him, let alone insisted on it. What he should have done was to tie her up again, good and tight this time, and mail her back to Philadelphia. He smiled at the image, thinking that he wouldn't want to be the person who opened up *that* box.

But he *had* insisted she stay, just as he'd insisted she come to dinner with him tonight at Lucas and Julianna's. She argued heatedly over that, too, insisted she'd be intruding on a private get-together. But in the end, he'd won that round, too, and now, deep in a conversation with Maggie, she sat beside him at the dinner table.

He had to admit she looked pretty tonight. She'd worn a rose-pink silk blouse and tucked it into the narrow waist of her tailored white slacks. She'd done something different with her hair, brushed the sides away from her face and clipped them together in the back. The style emphasized her high cheekbones, and the touch of cosmetics she'd applied to her eyes made them look wider, softer. If a man wasn't being careful, it would be easy to drown in those eyes. But of course, *he* was being careful. Very careful.

He just felt some strange, twisted sense of obligation toward her. That was the only reason he'd insisted she move into his cabin and come to dinner with him, he reasoned. She was here in Wolf River because of him, and he simply wanted to see her get back home in one piece.

He'd made inquiries into the occupants of the other cabins, but so far, no one was suspect. The honeymoon couple had checked into their cabin before Cara had even arrived, the father and son appeared legitimate, and the other two cabins rented were locals. Whoever was following her was hiding well.

But whoever was after her, wouldn't stop here. Ian knew they'd follow her back to Philadelphia, and once she left Wolf River, there was nothing he could do to protect her.

But someone else could. He'd already made a phone call that would ensure she'd be taken care of once she returned home. But she didn't need to know about that right now.

She'd find out soon enough, and she wasn't going to like it one little bit.

In the meantime, he wasn't going to let her out of his sight. He almost laughed at the irony of it all.

"Hello. Earth to Ian. Would you like some carrots?"

"Huh?" He blinked, then realized that Julianna was speaking to him from the other side of the Blackhawk dining room table. "Oh, sure. Thanks."

"You look like you got a bone stuck in your craw, Shawnessy. Hey, Cara," Lucas said from his place at the head of the table, "maybe you should slap him hard on the cheek, just in case."

"I think you're supposed to punch him in the stomach," Nick offered. "Makes that bone shoot out like a missile."

"Really?" Drew, Nick's five-year-old son asked excitedly. "Can I watch?"

Ian shook his head at their nonsense, while Maggie and Julianna rolled their eyes. Cara laughed, and in spite of himself, he couldn't help but think that the sound was like music.

Shocked that he would even have a thought like that, Ian frowned darkly. Good Lord, all this hearts and flowers stuff surrounding him must be rubbing off. He speared a big bite of carrots and concentrated on the food rather than the enticing scent of raspberries drifting from Cara.

"Thank you all for allowing me to join you tonight," Cara said, and looked at Lucas and Julianna, then Nick and Maggie. "I know this was a special celebration. I hope I haven't intruded."

"We're glad you could join us." Maggie glanced at Nick, and the tender look they exchanged baffled Ian. Seeing Lucas take the fall was bad enough, but Nick... Geez, what was the world coming to?

"We'd love to have you come to the wedding tomorrow, as well," Maggie added with a smile. "In fact, we insist."

Cara shook her head. "I couldn't impose on you like that."

"She'll be there," Ian said flatly.

Her cheeks flushed pink. "I appreciate the offer, really, but I didn't bring a dress on this trip."

"What's wrong with what you've got on?" Ian ladled some gravy on a big mound of mashed potatoes. "It looks fine."

"So like a man." Julianna sighed with exasperation. "Don't worry about a dress. We're about the same size, at least, I used to be your size—" she glanced down at her twins sleeping in their carriers beside her chair, then smiled. "Everything's so snug now I may have to hire Omar the tent maker to redo my wardrobe."

Lucas took his wife's hand and kissed it. "You looked damn good last night in that—"

"That's enough, Lucas. There's a child present." Julianna's face turned bright red.

"I'm not a child." Drew pouted while he shoved carrots under a pile of potatoes. "I'm going to be in kindergarten."

Maggie patted her son's hand. "Aunt Julianna was talking about your father, dear."

Julianna smiled and turned back to Cara. "Don't worry about a dress. I have something that's perfect for you. After dinner we'll go upstairs and you can try it on."

Cara started to open her mouth to protest, and Ian flashed her a dark look. She pressed her lips tightly together and smiled. "Thank you," she said to Julianna. "That's very nice of you."

"Ian says you're from Philadelphia," Maggie said. "Do you have family there?"

"My parents both passed away, but I have four brothers." Cara sipped on a glass of red wine. "Gabe's the oldest and most serious. He scowls a lot, but he's really a pussycat. He actually reminds me a lot of Ian."

Nick and Lucas barked with laughter, while Maggie and Julianna pressed their napkins to their mouths to hide their smiles. Ian glared at them all.

"See," Cara said sweetly and looked straight at Ian. "Isn't that furrow in his brow adorable?"

"Just the word I would have used," Lucas said, struggling to control himself. "What do you think, Santos?"

"No question, he's adorable," Nick grinned at Ian. "What do you ladies think?"

Both Maggie and Julianna nodded. "Adorable," they both said at the same time.

"I think so, too," Drew added, giggling.

Eyes sparkling, Cara looked at Ian and smiled wide. Ian decided that she no longer had to worry about anyone killing her. He was going to do the job himself.

"Then there's Callan," Cara went on when the laughter finally quieted down. "He's the quiet one, but intense. Lucian is next, he's the hothead, but cools down as fast as he explodes. And Reece, well, he's always cheerful unless you make him mad. Not an easy thing to do, but I've managed to master the ability."

Ian already felt a kinship with at least one of her brothers. He knew firsthand that Cara Sinclair could turn the calmest man into a raving madman.

"Your family sounds wonderful," Maggie said while cutting a piece of roast into bite-size pieces for her son. "Maybe we'll get to meet them one day."

"Philadelphia is a great city. Everyone should go there at least once in their life." She swiveled a glance at Ian. "Don't you think so?"

"There are a lot of places a person should go once," Ian said. "And some places a person shouldn't go at all."

"Well, a person wouldn't know they shouldn't go, unless they went." She aimed a smile at him. "Would they?"

Ian started to respond, but little Drew spoke first. "Uncle Ian told my Daddy that he's going to Guyro next week for three months," the boy said around a bite of roast. "Is that far?"

The room went quiet and everyone exchanged quick glances. Cara looked up, then lifted a brow as her gaze settled on Ian. "Guyro?"

"Cairo." Damn, he thought Drew had been absorbed in a video game on the TV when he'd been talking to Nick and Lucas in the den earlier. "I have business there."

"You export cellular phones to Cairo?"

"I'm considering the possibility."

"You're going to *Cairo,* for three months, to *consider* selling phones there? And you never mentioned this to me?"

Ian shifted uncomfortably under Cara's narrowed gaze. If this went any further, it would look like a lovers' spat. Hell, it already did, he thought with irritation.

But nobody here knew who Cara really was, or why she

was here. And this most certainly wasn't the time to tell everyone. He hadn't even decided yet *if* he was going to tell them at all. Let them assume she was upset he was leaving because she cared about him, he decided. What difference did it make, anyway?

He smiled at Cara, a slow, knowing smile that only lovers share, then leaned over and kissed her cheek. "Will you miss me, darling?"

Green flames shot from her eyes, but she forced a smile. "I was looking forward to showing you a few sights in Philadelphia. One in particular, that won't always be there."

"I think we should *all* go," Drew said around a mouthful of potatoes. "Families are supposed to take trips and be together."

Cara's smile widened, and she held his steady gaze. "From the mouths of babes," she said softly.

It's a conspiracy, he thought with a sigh, deciding to keep silent while everyone chatted about the wedding plans tomorrow. Hell, every time he opened his mouth, it got him into trouble, anyway.

When they finished eating, Lucas suggested cigars on the patio, but Julianna shook her head.

"Later, sweetheart. Maggie and I are taking Cara upstairs, and you boys have dish duty. We'll have coffee and dessert when we come back down."

Dish duty? Ian grinned at Lucas, who seemed to take Julianna's order in stride. He was already stacking dirty plates. And damn if Nick wasn't helping.

Not this boy, Ian thought, and started to back out of the dining room.

"Ian."

Julianna stopped him. She'd scooped up one tiny pink

bundle in one arm, and a blue bundle in the other. "You've got baby detail."

Before he could get a word out, she'd deposited one baby in each of his arms, kissed his cheek and ushered the women upstairs. Lucas and Nick grinned at him, then hustled out of the dining room, their arms full.

Alone. They'd left him alone. With *two* babies.

Panic slammed into his ribs. He couldn't breathe. Not this, anything but this. He'd disarmed a terrorist's bomb in Sudan, jumped from airplanes at thirty thousand feet into enemy territory, been shot at too many times to remember. And that all seemed like a piece of cake next to holding these little bundles in his arms.

Desperate, he looked up and saw Cara watching him from the doorway.

"You look a little pale, Shawnessy." A smile touched her pink lips. "Something wrong?"

"I—" He had to clear his throat. "I don't do this."

"Do what?"

"Babies," he croaked.

"But you are," she said sweetly. "And a fine job you're doing."

"Couldn't you...can't you..." He was too scared to move, but his look implored.

"Sorry. My hands are full. Unless, of course..."

"Anything," he pleaded. "Just name it."

"Anything?"

Knowing exactly where this was headed, he frowned fiercely. "You're a wicked woman, Sinclair."

She laughed at that. "Compliments will get you everywhere, darling. See you for dessert."

When she turned on her pretty heels and walked away, he almost caved in and told her he'd go to Philadelphia with her.

Damn woman!

Sweat dampened his brow as he stared at the babies in his arms. They couldn't weigh more than a feather each, their bodies were hardly bigger than his hands. The blue bundle was sleeping, but the pink one was wide awake. Her eyes, surrounded by thick, dark lashes, were big and blue, her skin the palest pink. She smelled brand-new, clean and freshly dusted with powder. She yawned a tiny perfect little O with her tiny perfect little lips, then looked right at him with her great big eyes and smiled.

His chest felt strange, like he'd swallowed a balloon. The baby smiled again, this time adding a soft little cooing sound, and the balloon inside him swelled.

He blinked several times, then glanced around. When he was certain he was alone and no one was watching, he looked back at the fragile little bundle in his arms and surprised himself by smiling back.

This time she not only smiled, she laughed.

God help me, he thought miserably, and sank down on a dining room chair. For the first time in his life he envied another man.

Eight

When the phone rang the next morning, Cara fumbled blindly for the receiver on the table beside the sofa. She'd argued with Ian the night before over where she would sleep—on the bed or the couch. But despite his desire to always have his own way, she'd held her ground until he'd finally stomped off to bed. It was a small victory, but when it came to Ian, her pride needed every stroke it could get.

She heard the sound of the shower running as she picked up the receiver on the third ring.

"Hello?" she mumbled, then buried her head under her pillow to block out the light.

"Who is this?" The question was clipped, the voice distinctly feminine.

Cara started to ask the same, then realized she was in Ian's cabin, answering his phone. And the woman at the other end of the phone sounded extremely irritated.

"Ah, this is Cara Sinclair." She sat, dragged a hair through her hair. "I'm a friend of Ian's."

"Tell Ian that Kelly Jordan is on the phone and I need to speak with him right away."

Well, she certainly was bossy, Cara thought, and made a rude face at the phone. Somebody certainly needed to teach this woman a few manners.

She glanced at the bathroom door, heard the squeak of the shower faucet as it was turned off. Definitely bad timing.

"I'm afraid he can't come to the phone right now, Miss Jordan," Cara said in her most secretary-efficient tone. "But I can take a message, or have him call you back when he's free."

There was a muffled oath at the other end of the line. "You tell Killian Shawnessy that he better call me back immediately or I'll—'

The phone was suddenly wrenched from her hand. Ian stood beside her, wearing nothing but a towel around his lean hips.

"Dammit, Jordan, I told you I'd call," he barked into the phone, then softened his voice as he glanced at Cara. "I'll explain later, but I can't talk now."

Cara told herself it was the surprise of Ian's sudden appearance that prevented her from tearing her eyes away. But for goodness sake, where *was* a girl to look when a man like Ian was standing two feet away, practically naked?

Certainly not at the floor.

Water still dripped from his hair onto his powerful shoulders, then down his broad chest until it disappeared into the edge of the white towel slung low around his lean hips. His legs were long and muscled, sprinkled with the same dark hair that covered his chest and dropped like a V over his flat stomach.

Her heart lurched, and though propriety dictated she look away, she couldn't. Besides, she wasn't shy about the male physique. She had four brothers, and had also spent two years on her high school swim team where Speedos left little to the imagination. She considered herself an expert judge on the configuration of the male anatomy.

And Killian Shawnessy was one fine configuration.

He spoke briskly into the phone, then hung up and turned to her. "That was Jordan," he said hesitantly. "One of my...business associates."

Jordan. Cara remembered the name now. When she'd phoned Ian two nights ago, after she heard someone at her front door, he'd called her Jordan. Her heart sank. Business associates didn't call at 2:00 a.m.

"It's none of my business who she is." She didn't dare look anywhere but at his face. "I apologize if my being here causes any problems for you."

"It's not like that. Jordan is, well, Jordan is just Jordan." He dragged a hand through his wet hair, then took a step toward her. When her eyes widened at his approach, he glanced down at his attire, or more accurately, lack of attire, and stopped. "Look, Cara, it's not what you're thinking."

"I'm not thinking anything."

But she was. She was thinking plenty. About the clean masculine scent of his body, about the towel draped loosely around his hips, if that towel just happened to slip away...

"Umm, if you're finished with the bathroom," she said a little too breathlessly, "could I get in there for a few minutes?"

But she didn't move.

"Sure."

He didn't move, either.

The annoyance that had been in his eyes only a moment before quickly turned to something else. Something deeply erotic and incredibly electric.

They stared at each other; the tension in the air tightened around them. Her entire body responded to his closeness. Her heart pounded, her breathing turned shallow, her skin felt tight.

When he reached out to her, Cara knew she should run, but it was impossible to move. He touched her face, skimmed her cheek with his hand, then brushed his thumb over her lips. With a will of their own, her eyes slowly closed, and she leaned into his touch.

"Is there anything you need?" he asked softly. "For the shower…?"

He moved closer still, so close she could feel the heat of his body…

The phone rang again.

She jumped. On an oath Ian pulled his hand back and snatched the receiver. Cara took the opportunity to scramble off the couch and head for the bathroom.

"No problem, Nick, it's fine," she heard Ian say tightly. "You didn't catch me at a bad time."

She paused at the bathroom door, slowly looked back over her shoulder. Ian turned at the same time, and their eyes met, held for one long, heart-stopping minute.

Before her knees gave out, before her pride completely disintegrated, she quickly shut the door and locked it.

Ian stood at the front of the small church beside Nick and watched Maggie float down the aisle on her father's arm. The wedding march poured from the church organ, and huge bouquets of flowers scented the warm late-afternoon air. Several ladies dabbed at their eyes, while Madge, clutching a tissue to her generous breasts, sobbed loudly. Beside her, Walt stretched his thick neck and pulled at his tie.

He knew exactly how Walt felt, Ian thought. His own collar felt three sizes too small. The only thing that made him break into a sweat faster than babies were weddings.

But hey, he'd take a bullet for Nick or Lucas, just as they would for him. If Nick wanted him to stand up here looking trussed-up like a turkey on Thanksgiving, then that's what he'd do. Still, Ian thought as he shifted his weight and twisted his neck, a bullet somehow seemed easier.

Maggie was halfway down the aisle, a vision in white lace, when another vision sitting in the center of the church on the end of a pew caught his eye.

Cara?

He'd dropped her off at Julianna's house before coming to the church with Nick and Lucas. She'd been wearing faded jeans and a white, V-necked sweatshirt. Now…good Lord, now… He had to swallow the lump in his throat so he could breathe.

Staggering was the word that came to mind. The dress, a slim-fitting, spaghetti-strapped number in deep, smoky green was a perfect match for her eyes. She'd swept her hair up into a mass of loose, tousled curls, revealing her long, slender neck. She wore a pearl choker, and he had a sudden image of her naked, wearing only that damn choker.

As if she could read his thoughts, Cara suddenly glanced at him. He could see the color rise on her cheeks, but she kept her gaze steady with his. Even as Nick took Maggie's hand and turned to the minister, Ian couldn't look away from Cara.

When the minister said, "Dearly Beloved, we are gathered here…" Ian forced his attention back to the ceremony, listened as Nick and Maggie exchanged vows, smiled when Nick's voice shook slightly.

When Nick and Maggie shared their first kiss as man and wife, the church broke into applause and whistles. Ian couldn't help but grin at the happy couple.

And as he watched them walk back down the aisle, he did his best to ignore the odd sense of foreboding that tingled at the base of his neck.

The reception was in the formal ballroom of the Four Winds Hotel, Wolf River's biggest and most elegant hotel, owned by none other than Lucas Blackhawk. White linens, tied with bows of tule and pink ribbon, draped the dozens of round tables, and the tall centerpieces were bursting with sprays of tiny white flowers and deep pink roses. Music drifted from the dance floor, a slow song dedicated to Nick and Maggie, and a deejay droned on about all lovers joining them on the dance floor.

Ian stayed close to the bar.

"That's one mighty-fine-looking woman you got there, Shawnessy." Lucas grabbed two bottles of beer from the bartender and handed one to Ian. "Mighty fine."

Ian took a long, deep swig from the bottle, then leaned back against the bar and frowned as he watched Cara glide around the dance floor in the arms of Brett Rivers. From the way she'd danced every dance since the music had started, it seemed that every eligible man here tonight—and a few not-so-eligible—agreed with Lucas.

He hadn't realized just how incredibly long her legs were until he'd seen her in that dress. How narrow her waist was—just the right size for a man's hands. Or how graceful the curve of her shoulders and back. How sexy.

Ian's hand tightened around his beer as Brett slid his hand lower on Cara's slim, smooth back. When the man said something close to her ear, she laughed. Ian clenched his jaw.

Lucas took a swig of his beer. "That Brett's a good dancer, don't you think?"

Ian knew that Lucas was goading him, but he refused to rise to the bait. He'd never been the jealous type, and he had no reason to be now, he told himself. He and Cara weren't involved. He just felt a certain…responsibility, that was all.

They were both leaving tomorrow, going their separate ways, and he couldn't rest until she was safely on a plane to Philadelphia. Once she was back home, he was certain he'd have nothing to worry about. She'd be fine. Absolutely fine.

When Brett pulled her closer, Ian thought he heard the bottle crack in his hand.

"Smile!"

A light flashed in his face, blinding him for a moment. Julianna grinned at him over the top of a throw-away camera. In spite of himself, Ian did smile, even if it was a little late.

"Good thing you married this gorgeous woman, Blackhawk, or I'd find it my bachelor duty to hit on her."

"Try it and you're a dead man," Lucas snarled goodnaturedly. "She's all mine."

Ian watched with amusement as Lucas pulled Julianna into his arms and gave her a kiss. They shared a look that had Ian tugging at his bow tie. There it was again, that strange prickling at the back of his neck. If he believed in them, he'd say it was a premonition of something coming.

But that was ridiculous.

"Cara looks wonderful in that dress, don't you think so, Ian?" Julianna took a glass of champagne from a passing waiter.

"It's nice," he said blandly, watched with irritation as Kirk Jensen, another single male, cut in on Brett when the deejay switched to a disco song. He felt some satisfaction that Kirk wasn't holding her close, but the way Cara moved her body was enough to make a man's brain melt.

"Nice?" Julianna raised a brow at Ian, then looked at Lucas. "He thinks she looks *nice?*"

"He's got it bad." Lucas gave his wife a knowing nod. "Real bad."

"Shut up, Blackhawk," Ian snapped. "You don't know sh—anything," he finished politely for Julianna's sake.

"Who's got it bad?" Nick came up from behind, signaled the bartender for a beer, then grinned at Lucas. "Oh, you must be talking about Ian."

Ian glared at Nick. "Just because it's your wedding, Santos, don't think I won't punch you out. Both of you."

Nick and Ian looked at each other and grinned. "*Real* bad," they both said at the same time.

That did it. Ian slammed his beer down, and since Lucas started it, reached for him first.

"Hey," Julianna said sharply, "isn't that Gerckee dancing with Cara? Nick, did you invite *him?*"

"We invited his parents," Nick said with a sigh. "He just showed up with them."

Gerckee? Ian's head snapped up. *Roger* Gerckee? And he was dancing with *Cara?*

A muscle jumped in Ian's jaw. Not in this lifetime, he thought, narrowing his eyes as he made his way to the dance floor.

"You must be new to Wolf River," the blond man said to Cara as he pulled her into his arms. "I would have noticed a woman who looks like you."

Cara wished that the dance had been fast instead of slow. This guy's hands left her cold, just like his pickup line.

Until now, she'd enjoyed dancing, though the one man she'd wanted to ask her hadn't come within a mile of her. And though her mind knew that was for the best, her heart didn't much seem to care.

"My name's Roger." Roger cocked his head and gave her a half smile, a look he'd obviously spent a great deal of time perfecting in the mirror, Cara decided. "Roger Gerckee. I'm a lawyer with Milton, Mead and Burns."

"How nice." She gave him a polite smile. "Are you friends with the bride or groom?"

"Both, actually." He spun her awkwardly, and Cara stumbled into him, another move he'd obviously practiced, she thought irritably. "We're school chums, though Maggie was a couple of years younger. We all hung out together. How about you?" he asked, bringing his face close to hers. "You here with someone, or do I have you all to myself?"

"She's with me, Gerckee. Hands off."

Cara had been so focused on avoiding Roger's sudden moves, and his hand that had dropped so close to her rear end, that she hadn't seen Ian come up. His heated stare drilled into Roger, who immediately dropped his hands as if he'd been burned.

"Hey, Ian, heard you were back." Roger shifted uncomfortably. "Long time no see. How's it going?"

"Fine."

Cara sucked in her breath as Ian scooped her into his arms and pulled her back onto the dance floor, leaving Roger behind, talking to himself.

"That was rude," she said in her most proper Miss Manners tone.

"You should be thanking me." He smiled tightly at

Madge and Walt, who danced by, cheek-to-cheek. "I saved your butt from that jerk."

Quite literally, Cara thought. "I thought he was sweet."

When Ian choked, she slid her arm over his shoulder and patted him on the back. "And very good-looking, too," she added. *If you go for the Lounge Lizard types.*

"Sweet, huh? Good-looking?" He studied her for a moment, then raised one dark brow. "Well, how 'bout we just dance right back over there and I give you back to him?"

She slid her other arm around him, leaned in close and whispered in his ear, "Do it and you die, buster."

He laughed softly in her ear, and she felt his body relax against hers. He pulled her closer, held her tight as they swayed to the music, a slow, sexy song about love and seduction.

She rested her cheek on his chest, wondered if she was the cause of his heart beating so heavily against her ear. Her own heart was beating fast, and her bones felt soft.

"So why do you dislike Roger so much?" She sucked in a slow, deep breath as Ian's hands slid down to the small of her back. "Did he steal your girl in the seventh grade?"

"Roger was a bully," Ian said dryly. "He tormented all the girls."

"You're a bully." Cara brushed her fingers over his collar and through the ends of his hair. "And you torment women. Especially me."

He sighed and pulled her closer. "Not half as much as you torment me, sweetheart."

Cara had the distinct feeling he wasn't teasing, and that his words spoke of a torment that had nothing to do with her badgering him to come to Philadelphia. He spoke of something deeper, and of a distinctly sexual nature.

That was there between them, she acknowledged. It had been there from the beginning. She'd tried to deny it, then tried to ignore it. But neither approach was her style. She'd always faced her problems head-on. And that's exactly what Ian was, she thought with a sigh. A problem.

A very big one.

She refused to think about that now. She was having a good time. Whatever came tomorrow, she'd deal with that head-on, too.

When several guests clinked their glasses with silverware, signaling for the dancing bride and groom to kiss, the entire room cheered them on. When little Drew ran over to his mom and dad, they picked him up and kissed him, too.

Cara looked up at Ian and saw him watching Nick and Maggie and Drew. "You don't get it, do you?" she asked.

He glanced back at her. "Get what?"

"All this. Weddings, marriage, children."

"What makes you say that?"

She smiled. "You have an expression of complete bewilderment on your face when you look at Nick and Maggie, or Lucas and Julianna. You're baffled by it all."

"That's ridiculous." The song switched to a livelier beat, but he still held her close. "They're my best friends. I'm happy for them."

"Of course you're happy for them," she said. "But you don't understand it."

He shrugged. "Maybe I'm just a little surprised, that's all. Lucas was always driven by his work. Nick was, well, Nick wasn't the type to settle down."

"And what type is it that settles down?" she asked.

He thought about that for a moment. "Dependable, reliable. Safe." A smile slowly tipped up one corner of his mouth. "Simpleminded, impulsive. Illogical."

She lifted one brow. "And you're none of those things, of course."

"Of course."

She opened her mouth to respond, but he twirled her sharply, then dipped her back. She couldn't help but laugh at his unexpected playfulness, and when he pulled her back into his arms and held her close, she allowed herself to relax, gave herself up to the moment and the pleasure of being in his arms without arguing.

She snuggled against him, breathed in the spicy scent of his aftershave and the red carnation in his boutonniere. His chest felt solid under the palms of her hands, and the heat of his skin drifted through his tuxedo into her fingertips, up her arms and through her body.

She wasn't certain when the warm, relaxed sensation curling through her body shifted to something else. Something tighter, something sharper and intense.

He felt it, too. She was certain of it. The tension wound itself like a living thing around them, coiled like a snake, vibrated like an electric current. His hands were warm on her back, his fingers rough and callused on her bare skin. She was certain it was accidental, but his lips brushed her temple. She shuddered involuntarily, then cursed the longing that shimmered through her body.

They were surrounded by other couples, but Cara felt as if they were the only two people in the room, in the world.

For at least thirty seconds.

She felt herself wrenched from Ian's arms and pulled into Lucas's embrace.

"My turn, Shawnessy." Lucas whirled her away. Ian frowned fiercely and started after them, only to be waylaid by a buxom blonde in the shortest, tightest red dress that Cara had ever seen.

"Uh-oh. MaryAnne's got her claws into him now." Lucas grinned broadly. "If he makes it out alive, Stephanie will most likely finish him off."

"MaryAnne?" Cara felt her own claws come out as the blonde slipped her arms around Ian's neck. "Stephanie?"

"MaryAnne Johnson and Stephanie Roberts. They hunt as a pack. One of them distracts and corners, then the other one pounces. Not a pretty sight. Ah, there comes Stephanie now."

Cara watched as a plump redhead in a low-cut, sequined gown bounced over to Ian and shrieked a welcome, practically pushing the blonde out of the way.

"You're supposed to be his friend." Cara tried not to laugh at the look of panic on Ian's face. "Why don't you go help him?"

"He's a big boy." Lucas turned her smoothly. "Besides, they'll keep him busy while we talk."

"Talk?" Cara looked warily at Lucas. "Talk about what?"

"About why both you and Ian have been lying to everyone." He kept his gaze steady with hers. "About who you really are and why you're here."

She stumbled, but he caught her and held her steady. She could lie, pretend she didn't know what he was talking about. But as she stared at him for a long moment, saw the concern in his dark eyes, the love, she knew she couldn't lie. He deserved better than that.

"I haven't lied about who I am," she said carefully. "I—we—only lied about having a relationship and about caring for each other." She glanced over at Ian, almost felt sorry for him as the two women both insisted on dancing with him at the same time.

She looked back at Lucas. "But as for the reason I'm here, you'll have to ask Ian that question. Only he can give you the answer."

Lucas nodded. "All right, that's fair enough. But you're still not being honest with me."

Confused, she frowned at him. "I don't understand."

"You said you were both pretending to care for each other, and that, my dear Miss Sinclair, is a lie in itself. You do care, very much. And so does Ian. He's just too stubborn to admit it."

She stared at him, too stunned to reply. Dear Lord, was it so obvious, at least on her part, that she'd fallen for Ian?

Because she had. Hopelessly and foolishly. And it seemed as though everyone else knew it, too.

She looked sharply at Ian; he was staring hard at her. She felt her cheeks flame. Did he know, as well? Did he think her one more silly bimbo who melted at the knees when he simply glanced her way?

"Excuse me." She stepped away from Lucas. "I think I need a little air."

He put a hand on her arm. "Cara, I'm sorry, I—"

Forcing a smile, she shook her head. "You and Julianna have been terrific, and I thank you for your hospitality last night. But I'll be leaving tomorrow after I pick up my car from Walt. Ian and I won't be seeing each other again after that."

When she spotted Ian making his way toward her across the crowded dance floor, she turned and headed in the opposite direction.

After tomorrow she'd have all the space she'd need between her and Ian, but for now the ladies' room would have to do.

Nine

It was past midnight when Ian parked the truck in front of the cabin. He'd considered spending the night at the Four Winds; Lucas had even offered rooms for both him and Cara. But Ian had wanted to spend his last night in Wolf River in the mountains. His next assignment would be a grueling three months, living in a one-bedroom apartment with two other men. It was going to be a long time before he'd see a pine tree or lake again, and he wanted to savor the last few hours he had left up here.

He glanced over at Cara, saw her staring wistfully out the truck window at the lake. A full moon shone down from a clear, star-filled sky and cast silver sparkles over the water.

"It's beautiful," she said softly.

You're beautiful, he thought. Moonlight washed over her face, emphasized the delicate curve of her cheek and jaw. Several golden curls tumbled loose from their pins and spilled onto her long neck. He ached to bury his hands into those silken strands, to taste her one last time.

Clenching his jaw, he got out of the truck and came around to open her door. She stepped out, and his gaze followed the slender curve of one leg, from her ankle all the way up to the hem of her dress, which had risen dangerously high on her smooth thighs as she slid from the seat.

He nearly moaned at the sight, and knew it was going to be a long night.

A chivalrous man would have offered his hand and helped her across the gravel walkway, but he was feeling anything but chivalrous at the moment. What he felt bordered on something closer to savage.

He heard the crunch of gravel as she trailed behind him, unsteady in her heels as she picked her way to the porch. The scent of pine filled the warm night air, and a chorus of frogs and crickets echoed off the lake.

Ian opened the door and held it for Cara, but she shook her head as she leaned against the porch rail and pulled off her shoes. "You go on. I think I'll stay out here a little while."

"I'll just say good-night, then."

"Good-night."

Turning, he stepped into the darkness of the cabin, barely able to control the urge to kick something.

"Ian?"

"What?" He hadn't meant to snap at her, but he had. When he glanced back over his shoulder at her, she stood facing him, a silhouette in the moonlight.

"Thank you for tonight. I had a nice time." She hesitated, and he saw her shoulders rise and fall with her sigh. "I'm sorry I've been such a bother to you, but I'm not sorry I came here. I'd do it all again in a second. Well, except for maybe the part when you tied me up and dumped me in the bathtub.''

He couldn't help but smile. "That was my favorite part.''

"Is that so?'' She pointed one high heel at him, and he was glad it wasn't loaded. "Mine was the look of sheer terror on your face when you were holding the babies. Imagine a big, strong man like you afraid of something so sweet and cuddly. I'll bet kittens and puppies make you shake in your boots, too.''

"They're right up there with half-naked women wielding frying pans,'' he added.

She laughed softly and shook her head, but remembering that night, and what had happened, took their light banter into another direction entirely, turned the mood into something completely different.

It felt as if the night air were suddenly pressing in on him, cutting off his breath, as if a steel band were closing around his chest, squeezing tighter and tighter.

He knew he had to leave. Now.

"Good-night, Blondie.''

"Good-night, Shawnessy.''

He made it to the doorway, then stopped. And turned back around to face her.

Her arms were at her sides, each hand holding a shoe. Her green silk dress shimmered in the moonlight, hugged her slender body like a second skin. He couldn't see her eyes, but he knew she was watching him. Waiting.

He moved slowly toward her, stopped inches away and stared down at her.

Somewhere, in the distance, a lone coyote howled.

"Cara,'' he whispered her name, heard the anguish in his own voice.

She sighed, lifted her face to his. "I know, Ian.''

He reached out, touched her cheek with his fingertips.

Her skin was so soft, so smooth. How he wanted this woman. Like he'd never wanted another woman before. The desperation he felt frightened as much as it angered.

"This won't change anything," he said tightly. "You have to understand that."

The shoes she held dropped to the porch. Her eyes closed as she pressed her cheek into the palm of his hand. "Just kiss me, Ian," she whispered. "Please."

Her quiet plea snapped the last of his control. He felt the low, strangled moan deep in his throat as he caught her mouth with his. She opened to him, met the forceful thrust of his tongue with her own velvet heat. Her arms wound around his shoulders and she clung to him, kissed him back with a passion that he'd known was there all along.

She tasted like chocolate and mint, a heady combination that had him deepening the kiss. He wrapped his arms around her and crushed her to him, frantic to have her closer. Her soft breasts pressed against his chest, made his blood race and his heart pound.

Lifting her off her feet, he carried her inside. His mouth never left hers as he kicked the door closed, then pressed her back against the smooth, hard wood.

The hunger for her gripped him painfully. His mouth slanted over hers again and again, and she answered, sliding her body sensually, erotically against his in a rhythm that matched the thrust of his tongue.

"Touch me," she demanded on a ragged breath. "I need your hands on me. Everywhere."

Her words inflamed him, seared his blood and pounded through his body. "Don't worry about that, darlin'," he said roughly, wanting nothing more than to do exactly as she asked, frustrated that he couldn't touch her everywhere at once.

He slid her dress upward, and she gasped when he

slipped his hands underneath. Her stockings ended at the tops of her thighs, held there by a band of lace and satin. The separation between cool silk and warm skin fascinated as much as it excited.

He pressed her firmly against the wall, slid his hands around her buttocks as he lifted her off the floor. He felt the soft texture of her lace panties under his rough fingers. "Wrap your legs around me."

She did as he asked, tightening her arms around his neck as she wound her long, sleek legs around his waist. Their bodies pressed intimately together, his arousal nestled firmly between her legs. On a moan, her head fell back against the door, and he nuzzled her ear while he slipped the thin straps of her dress off her shoulders.

Moonlight spilled in from the windows, casting a silver glow over the room. He could hear the distant hum of the refrigerator and the sound of their own heavy breathing.

"I've wanted you since the first moment I saw you." He felt her shudder when he nipped at her neck. "I thought I'd go crazy if I didn't have you."

"You have me." She sucked in a breath when his mouth moved downward to the soft swell of her breast. Her fingers raked through his hair. "You have me," she repeated, her voice hoarse and uneven.

Her surrender pleasured him on a masculine level as much as it did the physical. He wanted to possess this woman completely. Her mind, her body, even her soul. If only for this night, he wanted—needed—her to be his alone.

Because it was difficult to think, Cara simply let herself feel. The sensations hammered her: his callused hands on her skin, his hot mouth on her breast, the hard ridge of his arousal rocking between her legs. The tension coiled inside her, tighter, then tighter still, and she wondered if it were truly possible to die from the need burning inside her. When he nuzzled the silk neckline of her dress lower and clamped onto her nipple through the thin white lace of her strapless bra, she cried out and was certain that a person could in fact die from this much pleasure.

"Ian." She buried her fingers in his hair. "Please."

His mouth swooped back to hers, and he folded her in his arms, carried her into the bedroom. They made the long, dangerous fall to the bed together, rolled in each other's arms until he lay under her.

"Now I've got you where I want you, Shawnessy," she said in a breathless tease. "Don't you dare move."

The bedroom was bright with moonlight, and she could see him clearly. She straddled him, reached for the zipper at the back of her dress while keeping her gaze steady with his. His expression was fierce, his eyes narrowed and dark as he watched her.

She pulled the dress slowly over her head, let the silk slide soundlessly from her hand into a pool at the foot of the bed.

"Your hair," he murmured. "I want it down."

Lifting her arms, she tugged the pins loose and let her hair fall in a tumbled mass around her shoulders. With her eyes still locked to his, she reached behind her back and unhooked her bra. It fell to the floor with her dress. His chest rose and fell heavily as he stared at her. His face was like granite, his eyes smoldered. He started to reach for her, but she smiled softly and shook her head.

"Didn't I tell you not to move?" she reprimanded and pushed his hands back to his sides. "Now be still."

She started with the top button of his shirt, slowly worked her way down to the waistband of his trousers before sliding her hands back up again over his flat, hard stomach and broad, muscled chest. His body was like liquid steel, a warrior's body. Strong and powerful. Rugged. The realization that he was hers, completely hers, gave her a sense of power she'd never known before, made her brave and daring. A warrior's woman, she thought with a smile.

His hands clenched into fists at his sides when she pressed her lips to his chest, but he stayed still. She moved her mouth down, and the masculine, salty taste of his skin aroused her even more. She forced her mind to concentrate on giving pleasure rather than receiving, but the two were so intertwined it was impossible to stop the fire racing through her blood.

He had scars on his chest, she noted with curiosity. Several, in fact, giving the warrior illusion more substance than fantasy. She wouldn't ask. At least, not now. Whatever he'd done before, whatever had happened, she didn't want to know. There was only now, right now, and the two of them.

He squirmed when she kissed a long, jagged scar beside his navel. With her tongue she followed the line of his scar like a one-way road. To her delight, the scar continued below his waistband. She unbuttoned his slacks with every intention of exploring the path to its final destination, but when she tugged his zipper down over the hard ridge of his manhood, he gave a low growl, and suddenly it was she who was on her back.

She barely had time to catch her breath before his shirt was off, his shoes, then his pants, until he stood gloriously and magnificently naked. She was a tall woman, but she'd never felt so small, so vulnerable. Her heart jumped at the sight of him, pounded furiously in her chest.

He moved over her, slid his hands all the way up her legs to the top of her stockings, then slowly rolled each one down. His lips followed the path of his fingers, and he kissed the inside of each thigh, her knees, her calves, then back up again, until she writhed frantically under him.

His mouth ascended her body, tasting the curve of her hip, the flat hollow of her stomach, the underside of her breast. She bit her bottom lip to keep from crying out, but when he covered the hardened peak of her nipple with his mouth, she did cry out, arching upward at the jolt of intense pleasure that surged through her. His tongue was hot and wet; he drew her into his mouth and feasted hungrily on her. An ache spread through her body and centered between her legs, a pleasure that bordered on pain.

He moved to her other breast, gave equal attention there while he smoothed his palm over her hip, then her belly. His hand slipped under the lace of her panties, caressed the triangle of curls there before he slid one finger deeper, into the sensitive folds of her body, stroking her gently at the same time he took her breast into his mouth.

The assault on her body was more than she could bear. She moved urgently against him, raked his shoulders with her fingernails. "Ian," she gasped. *"Please."*

He needed no more encouragement. He slipped her panties off, then spread her legs as he moved over her. His entry was hard and fast, and she took him fully, lifting her hips to meet his. He made a sound, a deep, animallike sound and moved inside her. She wound her legs tightly around him, wanting him closer still.

The climax hit her like an explosion, and she nearly screamed from the force of it. She shuddered over and over, and he lifted her hips higher still while he thrust wildly. On a low, guttural groan, he shuddered, too, and she held on while they rode the intense waves together.

When he collapsed on top of her, his breathing ragged, his heart pounding, she smiled and gently slid her arms around his neck.

He had no idea what to say. Nothing like this had ever happened to him before. Never had he felt so out of control, so completely lost, so completely satisfied. In his entire life, nothing had even come close.

He started to rise, to ease his weight off her, but she wound her arms tightly around his neck and held him still.

"Don't move," she whispered.

"That's what you said before," he teased, "and look what happened."

There was a sparkle in her eyes when she looked up at him. "I know."

"You're an evil woman, Cara Sinclair. You frighten me."

She smiled at him. "Good."

She did frighten him, Ian thought suddenly. Like no woman ever had before. A strange sense of uneasiness came over him, but he shrugged it off and concentrated instead on the woman lying underneath him.

Moonlight edged her face in silver, and her hair spread out on his pillow like a silk fan. Her eyes were still heavy with passion, her lips swollen from his kisses. He brushed his mouth over hers lightly, gently nipped her bottom lip.

He knew he was too heavy for her, that she could barely breathe with him on top of her, but he couldn't bring himself to break the intimacy with her yet. Was afraid that if he did, nothing would seem real. And he needed this to be real. He needed her to be real.

He compromised by rolling to his back and bringing her with him. With a startled gasp, she hung on, then frowned at him while she raked her hair back away from her face. "You could have warned me."

"Just testing your reflexes."

"I'll have you know that I have excellent reflexes, as well as a keen sense of observation and an uncanny eye for details.'' She arched one brow and frowned at him. ''Maybe you weren't paying attention.''

''Paying attention to what?''

She tweaked a chest hair, and he grabbed her hand. ''Okay, okay.'' He rubbed at his chest. ''You've got great reflexes. Not to mention great legs, great arms, a great rear end—'' His gaze dropped to her breasts. ''And you've got terrific—''

''I get the picture.'' She folded her arms on his chest and covered the objects of his attention. ''You're not so bad yourself.''

''Yeah?'' He put his hands behind his head and gave her a cocky grin. ''Like what?''

''Well,'' she murmured, resting her chin on top of her arms, ''you have a nice nose.''

That wasn't exactly what he'd wanted to hear. ''A nice nose?''

''And cute ears.''

''You make me sound like a puppy.'' He frowned at her. ''That's the best you can do?''

She raised her eyes upward, as if she were thinking. With a low growl, he flipped her onto her back again. Laughing, she went with him easily.

''Maybe your powers of observation and attention to details aren't as keen as you think,'' he said huskily and slowly slid into her. ''Maybe we need to test them.''

''A test?'' She kept her gaze on his as she drew in a slow, trembling breath. ''Essay or multiple choice?''

He smiled slowly, eased himself out, then back in again. ''Definitely multiple,'' he said, and buried himself deep inside her.

It was still dark when she woke, though according to the clock on the nightstand, the morning was quickly approaching. She stretched, then reached out and found the bed empty beside her, the rumpled sheets cold. A brief, though sharp, sliver of dread pricked the back of her neck, then she saw Ian's open suitcase lying on the floor, filled with his clothes, and she relaxed.

He hadn't left. At least, not yet.

Yawning, she sat and pulled her hands through her tousled hair. She'd had very little sleep last night. Sleep hadn't been on her mind or Ian's. She'd never experienced anything like last night in her entire life. Not even close. And she knew she never would again. She knew that once they said goodbye, once she'd gone back to Philadelphia and he'd gone back to Washington, they would never see each other again. He'd made it clear what he thought of commitment and relationships. And when it came to Ian, Cara knew she could never settle for less.

What a fool she was to fall in love with Killian Shawnessy. A hopeless, stupid fool. She'd not only failed Margaret, Cara thought miserably, she'd also managed to break her own heart.

She was glad her brothers couldn't see her now. They'd all feel sorry for her, hug and fuss over her, and then they'd beat Ian up.

That thought actually cheered her up.

She dressed quickly, slipping on a pair of jeans and a white button-up shirt and boots, then went looking for him.

The cabin was empty. She looked out the window, saw the truck parked in front of the cabin, then spotted him down by the lake, standing at the water's edge.

She moved onto the porch, watched him from the railing. The sun was no more than a sliver of orange as it peeked out from the eastern ridge of mountains. The air was cool, filled with the fresh, clean scent of a mountain morning. She was going to miss this, she realized. The quiet, the peace, the sense that everything was right with the world, even when it wasn't.

He turned then, as if he knew she'd be there. His expression was somber as their eyes met. She waited, breath held, afraid that if he turned away from her she would fall apart right here.

He lifted his hand and reached out to her.

Relief poured through her. She walked to him, slipped into the arm he held out for her. He pulled her tightly to him, nearly lifted her off the ground as he kissed her long and deep. It was a goodbye kiss, she knew that, and she kissed him back with all the love and passion she felt for him.

His eyes were dark and narrowed when he pulled away and stared down at her, his jaw tight. She touched his cheek and smiled softly, wanted to talk about anything but what they were both thinking.

"Tell me how you ended up in the County Home for Boys," she said softly.

Her unexpected question softened the tension between them, which was exactly what she'd intended. He sighed, then tucked her into the crook of his arm and stared out at the lake.

"I punched out Hank Thompson, my seventh-grade history teacher," he said quietly. "The man had a big mouth, a little brain, and he couldn't keep his hands off his female students."

"Didn't the girls complain?"

"He was always careful who he preyed on. The weaker, shyer girls could be bullied into keeping quiet. A couple of the other teachers knew about it, but looked the other way rather than subject themselves to a lawsuit."

She thought of the young, frightened girls and felt sick to her stomach. "What happened?"

"I had to stay late one day, not an unusual occurrence. Some of my teachers felt that I exercised my individual right of expression more often than I should."

"You mean you had a bad attitude."

He smiled. "Something like that. Anyway," he went on and his smile faded, "that particular day I was getting my books out of my locker and I heard something, some kind of noise coming from Thompson's classroom. I wasn't even sure what it was, but I had a bad feeling. He'd locked the door, so I went into the classroom beside his which had a connecting door. It was unlocked."

He paused, and she could feel the anger tighten his body as he remembered.

"He had Mary Cook, another seventh-grader, pinned against the wall, his hands under her blouse. She had her eyes closed and there were tears on her pale cheeks. Thompson never saw me coming." Ian smiled tightly. "They told me later I broke his nose and jaw."

"You beat up an adult when you were in the seventh grade?" she asked incredulously.

"I was always big for my age. Plus I was mad as hell. That gave me an edge, too."

"But why did they send you to the County Home for Boys?" she asked. "Surely Mary and her family would have stood up for you."

Ian shrugged. "Mary begged me not to tell anyone the truth. She was too humiliated. And the only family she had was a drunk father who would have probably blamed her for Thompson coming on to her, then beaten her for it."

Cara closed her eyes and shook her head. "So you never said a word? You just let them send you away?"

"It didn't matter to me. The foster home I was in at the time was happy to see me gone, and besides, the Home is where I hooked up with Lucas and Nick, so something good did come out of it.''

At that moment Cara realized how much she'd taken her family for granted. She realized that there were countless children and people who had no one they could turn to when they needed help. Or love.

This was how Ian had been raised; his only family were two men who'd shared the same misfortune of being alone, without family. So they became family. They were all he knew, all he trusted. All he would ever let himself trust.

She loved him more than she would have thought it possible for one person to love another. But he didn't love her back. He didn't need anyone, didn't want anyone else in his life.

She wanted to curse at him, at the universe for playing such a cruel trick. She wanted to cry, to beg, to rant and rave and stomp her feet. Instead, she brought his face to hers and kissed him gently.

"What about Thompson?" she asked. "Was he ever caught?"

Ian nodded. "One of the parents found out what he'd been doing and a lynch mob showed up at the school one afternoon. Thompson was arrested, convicted on molestation, then sent to jail. They never admitted they made a mistake, but the courts released me from the Home the following week."

"Thank God there's some justice in this world," she said firmly. "I hope that man rots in jail for the rest of his life."

The shriek of a hawk echoed in the still of the morning, and they both watched the bird glide over the lake, searching for breakfast.

"We need to get ready to go," he said quietly. "Walt will be waiting for you to pick up your car."

She sighed, then nodded slowly, slipped an arm around his waist as they turned and headed for the cabin.

He stopped halfway there, lifted his head as he searched the area.

"What's wrong?" she asked.

"I don't know." He listened. "Just a feeling, but I'm not—"

The cabin exploded, cutting off Ian's words, and Cara felt as if an angry giant had backhanded her to the ground. She heard Ian shout her name as he covered her body with his, felt the sharp sting of fiery sparks on her face and hands. He dragged them both behind the truck, held her in his arms until the downpour of wood and debris settled into a light rain of ash and dust. The cabin was in flames, and the sound of fire eating wood replaced the quiet of only moments ago.

"Are you all right?" he asked, still holding her tightly.

"I—I think so." The world was spinning around her. Dazed, she put a shaking hand to one temple and sat. Her stomach clenched at the sight of blood on Ian's forehead. "You're hurt."

He shook his head. "It's nothing."

She brushed his hair away from his face, needing to touch him as much as she needed to reassure herself he was all right. The cut was superficial, but no doubt it would leave another scar.

What an odd thought, she mused. She'd nearly been killed and yet here she sat, contemplating the number of scars Ian had.

Her knees were shaking as they rose together and stared at the cabin. Black smoke billowed upward from the dancing flames. Ian's face was hard as granite as he stared at what should have been the end of both of their lives. There was something in his eyes she'd never seen before. Something cold and ruthless. Violent. She shivered at the icy chill slithering up her spine.

"Well, darlin'," he said tightly as he glanced at her. "Looks like you're twenty dollars richer."

Her head was still reeling from the blast, her ears ringing. "What are you talking about?"

He turned back to the cabin, and his dark eyes narrowed to angry slits. "We're going to Philadelphia."

Ten

Ian sat in the black sedan he'd rented at the airport and stared across the street at Margaret Muldoon's three-story brownstone. Thick maples lined the wealthy residential street; historic wrought iron lampposts now fitted with electric lights, rather than gas, brightened the dark sidewalks. Tidy, numbered mailboxes sat empty, waiting to be filled with the next day's mail.

Wolf River was a world away from here, Ian thought. A lifetime.

Cara slept curled up on the seat beside him. Considering the day they'd had—not to mention the night before, he thought with a smile—he was impressed she'd lasted this long, even though it was only eight o'clock. The father and son fishing up at the lake had reported the explosion to the fire department, and a fire truck had arrived within minutes to put out the flames. The department's initial report had been a faulty water heater.

Ian knew better, he'd sorted through the rubble himself and found the detonator for the bomb. But he'd pocketed the device and said nothing. He wanted to get himself and Cara out of Texas as quickly as possible, and if the sheriff were involved, it might slow them down. Ian had called Lucas, told him that he and Cara were all right and not to worry, then promised that he'd explain everything in a day or two.

The explosion had changed everything for Ian. There had been no way he could let her go home without him after that, no way he would let her out of his sight. He'd had to be sure she got home safely, had to know that she was all right.

He was certain that whoever was after Cara would follow her back here from Wolf River. Computers could trace every flight from Dallas to Philadelphia, starting from the day Cara flew into Dallas to the day she flew out. All he had to do was find a link, then a match. When you had friends in high places, it could be done, and if all went well, Ian expected he'd find his man within a day or two and still get back to Washington in time for his briefing.

Cara whimpered softly in her sleep, and he leaned over to brush her hair off her face. His jaw clenched at the sight of the scratch on her cheek. He told himself that when he found the bastard responsible, he'd rip him apart with his bare hands.

He sighed heavily, gently rubbed a strand of her silky hair between his fingers. Reluctantly, he admitted to himself that Cara had been right when she'd told him he didn't want anyone to matter to him, that it was easier not to care about someone. Safer.

But now he did care. About her. He cared like he never had for any woman before.

And he'd been wrong when he'd told her that making

love wouldn't change anything. It had. She'd touched a part of him no other woman ever had. His heart, and his soul. No matter what happened, she would always be a part of him.

"Hey, Blondie," he whispered in her ear.

She opened one sleepy eye. "We here?"

"We're here."

She amazed him. Any other woman would have been in hysterics, or gone to pieces after a day like she'd had. But she'd hung in there, was still hanging in there. She'd nearly lost her life; her clothes and expensive camera had been destroyed; and the only thing that had seemed to upset her was that Julianna's dress and shoes had been ruined.

There'd been no time to stop after picking up Cara's rental car from Walt, so they both still wore the same clothes they'd had on this morning. They smelled like smoke, and his flannel shirt had tiny black holes where flying embers had burned through. In general, they were both pretty ragged, but he thought she'd never looked more beautiful to him. He wanted to pull her into his arms and hold her, make love to her again and again.

But that, he thought with a sigh, would have to wait.

"If you'd rather, we could do this in the morning," he offered.

Shaking her head, she sat up and dragged her hands through her tangled hair. "Margaret's anxious to meet you. She's been waiting since I called her from the Dallas airport and told her you were coming."

He nodded and opened his door. "Let's do it, then."

The porch light was on over Margaret's front door. Cara paused and looked up at Ian, then reached for the shiny brass knocker.

Ian felt a strange twist in his stomach. His palms were damp. *I'm tired,* he told himself. That's all. Just tired.

A slender man answered the door. About thirty-six or seven, five-nine, Ian guessed. Short brown hair, thick, wire-framed glasses. Custom-made white button-up shirt and tailored black dress slacks. Manicured hands.

"Cara." The man smiled broadly.

"Hello, Peter." Cara returned the smile.

The man—Peter—pulled Cara snugly into his arms. A little *too* snugly, Ian thought irritably when he didn't release her right away. Ian felt his shoulders relax when the man finally stepped away.

"Good God, what's happened to you? Are you all right?" Peter took in Cara's rumpled appearance.

"I'm fine, but I'll explain everything later." She glanced at Ian. "Peter, this is Killian Shawnessy. Killian, Peter Muldoon, your cousin."

"A pleasure to finally meet you." Peter's smile was friendly, his handshake firm. "We've been waiting for you. Please, come in."

They stepped inside the entry. The floor was white marble, the staircase polished mahogany. Nineteenth-century paintings of Victorian life and landscapes covered the walls, and the scent of red roses on an oak entry table filled the air.

"Where's Margaret?" Cara asked as Peter led them through a set of double doors to the left of the staircase.

"She's been a bundle of nerves since your call this morning," Peter replied. "I thought she should rest in her room until you got here."

Cara frowned. "Has she been taking her medication?"

The room they entered was dark wood with hunter green carpet. Two leather chairs faced an antique desk, and a massive grandfather clock beside the fireplace ticked loudly.

"As long as I stand over her and watch. Even then, I

think she spits it out when I'm not looking. The woman is stubborn down to her toes.'' Peter smiled apologetically at Ian. ''Sorry. That's no way to introduce you to your grand-mother. I'll be right back.''

Ian glanced at Cara when Peter had left. She shifted rest-lessly, nibbling on her bottom lip. She was worried, he realized, and moved beside her. When she looked up at him, he cupped her chin in his hand. ''In spite of what you might think of me,'' he said softly, ''I'm not a heartless bastard.''

She gave him her first real smile since the cabin had exploded. ''Is that so?''

''Yeah. That's so.'' He rubbed his thumb along her soft cheek and was delighted at the light that sprang into her eyes. He wanted to see that light there again, later, with her naked body under his while he—

''Just like a Muldoon. Can't keep his hands off a pretty woman.''

At the sound of the woman's deep voice, Ian dropped his hand and turned abruptly.

She was tall, looked remarkably young for her age. She wore white linen slacks and a chocolate-brown silk blouse that matched the color of her eyes; sharp, clear eyes that moved over him, assessed him with quick intelligence. Eyes that felt strangely familiar. Her hair was silver, short and thick and swept back from her angular face.

She moved into the room, keeping her gaze steady with his, and that's when he noticed she had a cane, the only sign of frailty that Ian could see. She stopped two feet away and frowned suddenly.

''Why on God's Good Earth do you look as if you've been chewed up and spit out?'' she asked briskly. ''Are you homeless?''

He couldn't help but smile. "No, ma'am. But I'm afraid it's a long story."

"When you're old, all stories are long." Glancing at Cara, Margaret's brow furrowed deeply. "Are you all right, my dear? You look absolutely tattered."

"I'm fine." Cara smiled and moved into the embrace Margaret offered. "It's just been a busy day."

"Indeed." Margaret turned to Peter, who'd been standing by the doors. "Peter, take care of Cara while I speak with my grandson, will you? She looks as if she's starving. And ask Emily to make sandwiches and coffee and send them in here. We'll be occupied for a while."

Ian looked at Cara and nodded for her to go ahead. Still, when he watched Peter put his hand on Cara's back and lead her from the room, he felt a muscle twitch in his jaw.

"You needn't worry about Peter," Margaret said firmly when the door had closed. "He's tried every which way to catch that girl's attention, and she hasn't even blinked. It's going to take someone much more—" she hesitated "—robust, shall we say?"

The woman didn't miss a thing, Ian noted with a lift of his brow. "Mrs. Muldoon—"

"Try Margaret for now, see how that feels." Her eyes softened as she took his chin in her hand and studied his face. "You look exactly like your father, especially the eyes. Dark and dangerous and a little wild. But you have your mother's hair, the same color, the same texture. She was a beautiful girl. Only seventeen when you were born."

"You can't be certain your son was the father of her baby," Ian said.

She reached behind him and pulled a photograph from the mantel. "Oh, but I am."

The man in the photograph was younger, but they had the same chin and angular cheekbones, the same expression. And she was right about the eyes, too. It was like looking into a mirror, he thought in stunned amazement. They could have been brothers, twins, even.

Or father and son.

He stared at the picture, then slowly lifted his gaze to Margaret. He had to clear the tightness in his voice before he could speak. "I don't know what to say."

She smiled, then gestured to the chairs beside the desk. "Right now, let's just start with that long story of yours. Something tells me it's going to be fascinating."

After eating a light dinner prepared by Margaret's housekeeper, Cara asked Peter if he'd mind driving her home. She'd decided that it would easier for both her and Ian if there were no goodbyes. She couldn't imagine standing there shaking his hand while Margaret and Peter stood by watching. What would she possibly say? "Thanks, Mr. Shawnessy, it's been swell?"

She'd have ended up in a puddle at his feet, crying her eyes out like a baby. And that was one humiliation she couldn't bear.

Her goal had been to bring him to Philadelphia to meet his grandmother and cousin, and she'd accomplished that. What she needed to do now was put everything that had happened between her and Ian behind her and get on with her life.

And while she was at it, she might end world hunger and teach a pig to sing.

Sighing, she glanced over at Peter as he parked his Lexus in front of her apartment building and cut the engine.

"I can come up with you, if you like," he offered.

Cara saw the hope in Peter's eyes and wished she could feel even a little for him of what she felt for Ian. How easy that would make life. How simple. But she couldn't. It just wasn't there. "Thanks, but I wouldn't be very good company right now. Tell Margaret I'll call her in the morning."

She kissed his cheek, then got out of the car, glad that he hadn't insisted on coming up with her. Not that Peter would have insisted, of course. It simply wasn't in the soft-spoken man's nature to be pushy.

Unlike *some* men, she thought as she headed up the stairs to her second-story apartment. Some men—one in particular with the initials KS—were downright bullies when it came to getting their own way.

She'd had four big brothers telling her what to do her entire life, and she'd naturally rebelled. But for the first time, with Ian, she hadn't minded someone telling her what to do. In fact, she'd actually welcomed it. She'd been in a daze since the cabin had exploded, and she'd desperately needed someone to lean on. Someone to take charge. And he had, with a calm and a resourcefulness that had amazed her.

It was strange, she thought as she slipped her spare key from her hiding cubby behind a modified piece of door molding and opened her door. Strange just *how* calm and resourceful he'd been. As if he handled bombs exploding every day. Not to mention getting new ID and last-minute travel arrangements.

Very strange.

An odd sensation rippled through her, something she couldn't quite put her finger on, but she shrugged the feeling off and slipped her key back into its hiding place. She was tired, and it most certainly had been a long day. All she needed was a long, hot shower and a good night's sleep. First thing tomorrow she'd start a file search in her computer. By a simple process of elimination, she should be able to come up with a list of individuals who might be after her.

She sorted through the mound of mail her landlady had collected for her, then listened to her phone messages before heading to the bathroom where she stripped off her clothes and stepped into the shower. The water was hot, the blast strong, and she closed her eyes with a sigh as she dumped raspberry-scented shampoo over her head and scrubbed.

At the click of the shower door opening, Cara drew in a breath to scream, but gasped instead at the sight of Ian standing there.

"Damn you, Shawnessy!" She grabbed a bottle of conditioner and threw it at him. "You scared the hell out of me!"

"Sorry." He ducked the missile, then grinned at her and let his hot gaze slowly rake over her wet, naked body. "You deserve it for walking out on me without so much as a word."

"You needed to spend time alone with Margaret," she insisted, and as much as she wanted to know how their meeting had gone, this hardly seemed the time. She tried to cover herself with her hands, but when her efforts proved futile, she turned her back to him instead and glared at him over her shoulder. "Do you think we could discuss this later?"

He folded his arms and gave equal attention to her backside. "I want to discuss it now."

"Ian, I'm taking a shower, for God's sake!"

"Good idea." He dragged off his boots, then started to unbutton his shirt. "I'll join you and we can talk at the same time."

"I didn't ask you to join me." She watched him strip off his shirt, then unzip his jeans. Her knees went weak when he shoved the denim down. "And I don't want to talk, either," she snapped.

"Okay." He stepped into the shower and closed the door behind him. "We won't talk then."

He hauled her into his arms, buried his hands in her wet hair and dragged her mouth to his. His kiss was deep, hungry. Urgent. Desire pulsed through her veins as he pressed her back against the cool tile, thigh to thigh, torso to torso, skin to skin. The feel of his hard, powerful body against hers made her heart pound.

"Ian." She pulled her mouth from his, struggled to catch her breath. "How did you get in here, anyway? I know I locked my door."

He bent and nuzzled her neck while his rough hands moved over her shoulders, down her slick, wet sides. "Margaret gave me a key. When you didn't answer my knock, I let myself in."

"*Margaret* gave you a key?" she sputtered. "Margaret knows that you came over here?"

He raised his head and frowned at her. "Of course she knows. Where else would I be sleeping tonight?"

"At Margaret's, of course." She felt her cheeks burn, and as his hand rounded her bare behind, her blood burned, as well. "What will she think?"

"She's a very bright woman, Sinclair, and she's not blind." He lifted her hip to fit more snugly to his. "It's obvious we're sleeping together."

Cara groaned at that, or maybe she groaned because his hands had moved up to her breasts. "How will I face her? She sent me as her friend to find you, not seduce you."

His laugh was husky and deep. "Is that what you did, seduce me?" He kept his dark gaze on hers while his thumbs circled the hardened peaks of her breasts. "And here I thought it was the other way around."

"I let you think that," she said breathlessly, arching into his hands. "Male pride is such a delicate thing."

"Delicate?" He lifted her, pressed her tightly against the shower wall, then slowly brought her back down onto his arousal. "Surely you can come up with a better word than that."

Several came to her mind, not one of them was close to delicate. This man was strong and tough, virile. The dark stubble of his beard, the wild, intense look in his eyes, the hard, square set of his jaw. Everything about Ian was powerfully, incredibly male.

Steam swirled around them, hot water pounded their bodies. Shampoo still lingered on her shoulders, and the scent of raspberries filled the damp air.

She gasped his name, wrapped her legs tightly around his waist and held on to his wet shoulders while he moved inside her. Need, as sharp as it was urgent, shuddered through her. She wanted this man, only this man.

She loved him. With her heart, her mind, her soul. Nothing had ever felt so right before. She was certain nothing ever would again.

As if he'd read her thoughts, he went still. His breathing was ragged, his gaze intense. His hold on her tightened almost painfully as he stared deeply into her eyes.

"Cara," he whispered her name as he never had before. With such tenderness, she thought she might cry. But there were no promises, no words of love. She saw the sorrow in his eyes, knew that he wanted her to understand. He cared about her, but that was all he could offer.

And if that was all he could offer, then that's what she would take. But he'd never forget her, she resolved. She'd make certain that he remembered her, that every minute they were together would be etched in his memory.

She cupped his face in her hands, felt the scrape of his beard on her palms. "Kiss me," she demanded, and brought his mouth to hers.

Hot water sluiced over their joined bodies as he moved inside her, slowly at first, increasing the rhythm with each pleasure-building thrust. She moved with him, murmuring his name and trembling with need.

"Hurry." She dragged her nails over his strong, wet shoulders. "Please hurry."

The sound he made in the back of his throat was raw and wild, desperate. Her heart thundered in her head, and she felt as if she'd been turned inside out, with every nerve open and exposed. She held on tightly, clamped her body to his and rode the pleasure upward, higher, faster, until she reached the crest with a shattering cry.

His hands tightened on her; with a deep, guttural groan, he shattered, as well.

Eleven

He woke to the smell of coffee and the sound of traffic from the street below. Sunlight streamed in, hot and bright, through the lace curtains, blasting his face with the force of a laser gun. Groaning, he sat on the edge of the bed and scrubbed a hand over his face.

The bedroom came into focus after several moments, and he glanced curiously at his surroundings. It had been dark last night when they'd tumbled into bed, and he hadn't been interested in Cara's decorating scheme. He'd been much more interested in the room's green-eyed, long-legged occupant, and the feel of her body when he'd made love to her in her bed.

The walls were a pale pink, with a stenciled border of colorful flowers that matched the bedspread. Dried flowers spilled out of a basket on top of a white-washed pine armoire, and glass-framed water colors of English cottages and gardens brightened the walls. Everything about the room was feminine, including the delicate fragrance of lavender that drifted from a crystal bowl filled with pot-pourri.

"Good morning."

She stood at the bedroom door, wearing satin boxer pajamas the green of pistachios, a cup of steaming coffee in her hand.

"Morning."

Smiling, she crossed the room and handed him the mug. "Looks like you could use this."

"Only if it's thick as mud and black as grease." He took the cup and downed half of it. When the hot liquid began to seep into his bloodstream, he could have cried from the pleasure. "Woman, you do know how to bring a man to his knees."

"You mean to tell me that all I ever needed to get you here was a strong cup of coffee?" She cocked a fist on one satin-covered hip. "And to think of all the time I wasted up in those mountains trying to reason with you."

"It wasn't *all* wasted time." He smiled when her cheeks turned the same color pink as the roses on the bed sheets. "I never figured you for the pink floral type, Sinclair."

"There're a lot of things you don't know about me, Flash. And it's not pink. It's dusky mauve." Her gaze swept over his naked body, lingered where the "dusky mauve" sheets covered the middle part of his anatomy. "By the way, that color looks great on you."

He took another swig of coffee, then frowned at her as he set the mug on the nightstand. "Pink does *not* look good on me."

"Oh?" She arched one eyebrow. "So what color do you think looks good on you?"

"Green."

She gasped as he snatched her to him and rolled her

underneath him. "It looks good under me, too." He wiggled his eyebrows.

She laughed, but when he lowered his head to hers, she placed her hands on his chest and held him away. "Oh, no, you don't. You distracted me last night, but this morning we're going to talk."

He sighed, then rolled to his side and propped his head in his hand. "Talk about what?"

"You know perfectly well what." She sat, then blew her hair out of her eyes. "Tell me about Margaret."

"Margaret Muldoon?" He screwed up his face and thought. "Gray hair, brown eyes. Sharp as a tack and quick as a whip. I found out we also have a close mutual friend named Jack."

"Jack?" She stared incredulously at him. "Jack who?"

"Daniels." He grinned at her. "She's known him longer than me, though."

Her eyes widened as his meaning sank in. "Killian Shawnessy! Shame on you." She grabbed a pillow and smacked him with it. "Tell me you weren't drinking whisky with your grandmother."

"I didn't tell you. That would be breaking a promise."

"She can't drink with the medication she takes," Cara said firmly. "It's not good for her."

"That's why she doesn't take the medication." Ian slid his hand slowly up her smooth leg, only to have his fingers slapped. "Do you know you have a freckle behind your knee in the shape of an apple?"

She started to look, then frowned at him. "I do not. And stop trying to change the subject. The doctor told Margaret she needs to take those pills. They're for her blood pressure."

"She says there's nothing wrong with her blood pressure that a bottle of whisky and a few wild nights with a younger man wouldn't cure. She even asked if I had any older friends, someone around fifty or sixty."

She made a strangled sound. "I don't believe you. She just met you last night for the first time. How could she say all that to you?"

"She's seventy-eight years old, Blondie. She can say anything she wants. She also told me that when a person reaches her age, there's no time to pussyfoot around." He ran his hand up her thigh, watched her eyes turned smoky-green. "I happen to think that philosophy applies to any age."

She sucked in a breath when he slid his hand under the hem of her satin pajama top. She covered his fingers with hers, stopping him, but not pushing him away, either. "Are you going to see her again?"

"We're having lunch today. She wants you to join us."

She started to shake her head, and he said, "*I* want you to join us, too. If it wasn't for you, I wouldn't be here at all, remember?"

She stilled, then glanced down at their joined hands. "And how do you feel about that, Ian? About being here?"

The bedroom windows rattled when a large truck drove by on the street below, also setting off a car alarm and a slew of barking dogs.

Wolf River was definitely a lifetime away from here.

How did he feel about being here?

He understood that she wasn't asking about Margaret. She was asking about them. But he couldn't go there, couldn't give her, or himself, hope where there was none. He was leaving tomorrow, going back to the only life he knew, a life he could never ask her to share with him.

But there was now, and for the time they'd shared he would always be grateful.

"I'm glad I'm here." He curled his fingers around hers,

was amazed himself at the truthfulness of his admission. "But I haven't lied to you before, and I won't start now. You need something I can't give you, Cara. I wish I could, but I can't."

She looked away, but not before he saw the hurt. He didn't want it to be like this, dammit. He'd never wanted to hurt her.

"If you want me to leave now," he said quietly, "I'll understand. I don't want to, but if you say the word, I will."

He held his breath when she didn't answer, afraid she'd tell him to leave, afraid she'd ask him to stay. Either way he was doomed. It felt as if he were watching his life pass before him while he waited for her answer.

Relief poured through him when she finally looked back at him and smiled softly. "So how much time do we have before lunch?" she asked softly, and guided his hand to her breast.

Not enough, he thought as he covered her body with his. *Not nearly enough.*

"Where are my clothes?" Ian asked an hour later when Cara came out of the bathroom, showered and dressed. They both knew they'd be late for lunch if they showered together, so he'd been sitting in the kitchen, wrapped in her dusky mauve sheet, reading the paper and consuming a pot of coffee while he waited for her.

"I ran them down to the laundry room this morning while you were still sleeping." She smoothed her lime-colored cotton sweater over her short white skirt, then slipped on a pair of white flats. "I'll go get them while you shower."

"Dammit, Cara." He snapped the paper and tossed it on the table. "Someone's trying to kill you, and you're run-

ning all over the place without telling me. And you were
wearing pajamas this morning.''

''I put on my heavy overcoat and I took my pepper
spray.'' She walked over to him and kissed him on the lips.
''I appreciate the concern, but I'm a big girl, Ian. I can
handle this myself.''

He didn't think it was a good idea to tell her that he had
no intention of letting her handle it herself. She'd find that
out soon enough.

In the meantime he didn't want her out of his sight. It
was too dangerous.

''What do you mean, handle it yourself?'' he said tightly.
''We agreed you'd let the police take care of it when you
got back to Philadelphia.''

''*We* didn't agree to anything. I told you I'd report it to
the police when I got back, and I will. But I'm not going
to sit around while my file gets shuffled from one desk to
another. I have to go through my computer records, then
follow up on the leads.''

''Are you crazy?'' He stood, then grabbed at the sheet
as it started to fall. ''You can't go running around, chasing
after some lunatic. This guy means business, Sinclair. He's
not going to sit around and wait while you're running him
down. He's going to come after you, only next time it will
be face-to-face, and he won't bother to make it look like it
was an accident. He'll put a bullet in you from two feet
away, then walk away without looking back.''

Her face paled at his description. He hadn't meant to be
so blunt, but she was so damn stubborn, she left him no
choice.

''Well then,'' she said, lifting her chin, ''I guess I'll just
have to make sure he doesn't get that close, won't I?'' She
grabbed her pepper spray from a table beside her couch,
then headed for the door. ''I left a travel razor on the

counter in the bathroom if you want to shave after you shower. I'll be back in a minute with your clothes.''

''Cara! Get back here!'' He started after her, tripped on the damn sheet, then swore hotly when she firmly closed the door behind her.

He considered going after her, but a naked man in a pink sheet wouldn't scare a poodle, let alone a vicious killer.

Muttering curses, he moved into the living room and paced. He couldn't just stand here naked and do nothing while Cara might be struggling in the laundry room with a maniac. Adjusting the sheet, he turned toward the door, then went still at the sound of someone working the lock. Cara? He hadn't even time to move before the door opened.

It wasn't Cara.

Two men, both with dark hair, stepped into the room. Ian guessed them to be in their thirties, at least six foot three. One man wore a navy-blue polo shirt, the other a black T-shirt. With eyes narrowing to slits of green ice, they stared at him.

Damn.

It was the green eyes that gave their identity away. No question about it, these two were Cara's brothers. Ian gritted his teeth when they both took a long look at the sheet draped around his hips, then glanced back up at him.

''You Killian Shawnessy?'' the one in blue asked.

Ian nodded. ''You Gabe Sinclair?''

The two men studied each other for a moment. They didn't shake hands.

''This is Lucian,'' Gabe said after a moment. Ian met the younger brother's dark gaze, assessed the bend in his nose that suggested a previous encounter with someone's fist.

''Where is she?'' Frowning, Gabe looked around the apartment.

"Downstairs, in the laundry room. She just left."

"How much time do we have?"

"Maybe five minutes."

"Then I suggest you talk fast, Mr. Shawnessy," Gabe said. "Real fast."

She took longer than necessary, just to let him stew for a while. He'd started to sound like her brothers, for heaven's sake. He had no right to tell her where she could go or what she could do. He had no claim on her.

No claim at all.

Blinking away the threatening tears, she stomped up the stairwell carrying his clothes. His shirt was soft and warm from the dryer, and she pressed the cotton to her cheek, then breathed in the clean scent. Blast it, anyway. What was she being so sentimental for? That wasn't like her. She'd always learned to take her punches and still come out swinging. She refused to let this man turn her into some weepy, maudlin female.

So he didn't want her the way she wanted him, didn't love her the way she loved him. She'd get over it.

She would, she told herself as she pried open the molding to retrieve her key. It was gone. Had she forgotten to replace it last night?

She never forgot to replace her key. Look what he'd done to her, she thought, gnashing her teeth. Her brain was mush. Furious at that thought, she pounded on the door. "Open the door, Shawnessy."

When the door flew open, she threw the clothes at him.

"Hi, Sis."

Gabe? Her jaw went slack as she stared into her brother's eyes. Not *Gabe*. Didn't she have enough trouble without him showing up, too?

Ian. Oh God. She'd left him in nothing more than a sheet. *Casual,* she told herself. Just act casual.

"This isn't a good time, Gabe." She snatched the clothes back from him and brushed past. "Why don't I give you a call later and—

She stopped. Lucian leaned against the wall behind the door, arms folded while he stared darkly at her. *Not Lucian.* Anyone but Lucian. He was too much of a hothead to ever listen to reason.

She groaned out loud. This was a nightmare. A total nightmare.

Ian looked none too happy about it, either. He sat on the couch, his expression black against the pink sheet draped around his middle.

All three of them watched her. Ian, Gabe, Lucian. At least there was no blood, she noted. Yet.

The tension in the air, however, was thick enough to walk on. It wouldn't take much for a riot to break out. She thought about starting one herself, just to relieve her own frustration, but they'd just make a mess of her place, and she'd be the one who'd have to clean it up.

She tossed Ian his clothes and he disappeared into the bathroom, dragging the sheet behind him. Any other time, she might have laughed at the sight.

But this was hardly any other time. With a sigh she turned back to Gabe and Lucian. *Let's just get this over with.*

"Coffee, anyone?" she offered matter-of-factly.

Gabe scowled at her. "You have some explaining to do."

She scowled right back. "I'm twenty-six years old, dear brother. If I decide to have male company, that's nobody's business but mine."

"I'm not talking about him. We'll get to that later."

"We won't do anything of the—"

"Why the hell didn't you tell us someone was trying to kill you?"

Nothing he said could have as effectively taken the wind out of her sails. Mouth still open, she had to swallow the sudden knot in her throat before she could manage a word. "What did you say?"

"You heard him," Lucian said tightly. "You could have called us from Texas. We would have come and brought you back. At least met you at the airport."

"I didn't need anyone to bring me back or meet me at the airport." She looked from Gabe to Lucian. "How do you know about this?"

She turned abruptly at the sound of the bathroom door opening. Ian walked out, tucking his shirt into his jeans. She stared at him, then slowly narrowed her eyes.

"You told them," she accused.

He nodded. "They're your family. Cara. They can help you."

When you're gone, you mean, she thought with a mixture of heartbreak and anger. "When did you tell them?"

Her question surprised him. "I don't really see why—"

"This morning, when I was in the shower?" She shook her head. "No, they wouldn't have had time to get here this fast. So was it last night? After I left Margaret's?"

He shifted uncomfortably; she was certain she saw a muscle jump in his tight jaw.

"Cara—" Gabe started toward her.

Eyes snapping, she whirled on her brother. "Stay out of this."

With a shrug, he backed off. She turned to Ian. "Tell me."

He pressed his lips into a thin line. "I called them from Texas."

"From Texas?" she gasped. "You've known all this time that they were going to show up here, and you didn't tell me?"

"Of course I didn't tell you," he returned. "We all agreed—"

"Stop." She held up a hand. "Just stop right there. Don't even tell me what you 'all agreed.' I might have to hurt someone if you do."

She felt the thin thread holding together her shattered nerves begin to unravel, but she refused to break down in front of her brothers or Ian. That was exactly what they wanted, so they could step in and take over her life.

"Cara," Gabe said gently, but firmly, "come home with us. At least until we catch this guy."

She shook her head, drew in a slow breath to calm herself. "The only way for me to end this is to find out who's after me, and the answer has to be in my files somewhere. Once I have something, I promise you, I'll take it to the police. Until then, I'm not going anywhere."

"I told you she wouldn't listen." Lucian pushed away from the wall to move closer to her. "Let's do it my way."

Cara wasn't certain what Lucian's "way" was, but she was certain she didn't want to know. She also knew if this heated up to a shouting match, she wouldn't win. No one ever won a shouting match with Lucian.

"I know you're both concerned for me. I appreciate it, and I love you both for it." She moved to the door and opened it. "But we'll discuss it later. Right now, I need to speak to Ian. Alone."

Her brothers hesitated.

She stared them down. "I mean it. Both of you, out."

Lucian looked at Gabe, who sighed. When Gabe moved to the doorway and slipped her key back into place, Cara reminded herself to find a new hiding spot.

"We'll call you in an hour." Gabe kept his gaze steady with hers. "Just to be sure you're all right."

"She'll be at lunch with Margaret and me," Ian said.

"I'll be at my office." She looked right at Ian, dared him to argue, was almost sorry when he didn't. "Call me there."

Gabe looked at Ian, and something passed between them, some unspoken male understanding that she didn't like at all. In spite of everything, she kissed both her brothers, then shut the door in their faces before turning back to Ian.

"You had no right to tell them."

"Would *you* have?" When she simply pressed her lips together, he gave her a you-see-what-I-mean look.

"Listen, Shawnessy—" hands on her hips, she closed the distance between them and got in his face "—this is *my* life, *my* business. Just because we slept together doesn't mean you have any obligation or responsibility you have to fulfill before you waltz out of my life."

His eyes narrowed to sharp slits. "This has nothing to do with our sleeping together. And I never waltz anywhere, Blondie."

"Call it whatever eases your conscience then, buster, but I run my life and make my own decisions. I did just fine before you came along, and I'll do just fine after you're gone, which will be in about twenty-four hours from now."

She grabbed her purse from the coffee table, and with her shoulders squared, walked to the door. "Let's make it easy on both of us and just say goodbye now. I think it's best if you stay at Margaret's tonight. Tell her I'm sorry I couldn't join you for lunch, and I'll call her tomorrow."

"Dammit, Cara, you can't—"

"Yes, I can, Ian. You're the one who can't."

She closed the door, amazed that she was able to walk out on legs that were shaking so badly.

"Damn you, Killian Shawnessy," she said out loud, angry at herself for lying. She wasn't going to be fine, not now, not in twenty-four hours.

Not ever.

Twelve

"**Y**ou've reached Cara Sinclair's answering machine. She can't come to the phone right now, but leave a message and she'll call you back...

Beeep...

Ian stood beside the bed in Margaret's guest room, holding the phone tightly in his fist. "I've called six times," he shouted at the stupid machine. "Stop being so stubborn and pick up the phone! I know you're there, so pick up the *damn* phone. Cara, *Cara!* Dammit, *pick up the phone!*"

Beeep.

The machine cut him off.

Frustrated, more than a little angry, he slammed down the receiver.

He'd called her three times last night and three times this morning. He knew she was there; her brothers were keeping a close eye on her, following her to her office yesterday, then watching her apartment last night and this morning.

Gabe had told him that no one had come in and no one had gone out.

Damn the stubborn woman!

Dragging both hands through his hair, he glanced at the fax lying on the bedside table. It had come in over Margaret's machine last night from the Computer Resource Center at the Agency. There were six names on the list, four men, two women, who fell inside the circle of data he'd requested. But only two of the names interested him. One man, one woman.

The couple had flown into Dallas and rented a car the day before Cara arrived, then flown out the same day, on a later flight. A background check on their names brought up nothing, which meant they had something to hide and were doing it well. He had a damn good idea who they were, but until his source in Washington came up with photographs from fingerprints, he couldn't be sure. He just needed a little more time.

And time was something he didn't have.

His flight left in two hours, and if he drove straight from Dulles airport, he'd have just enough time to make it to his briefing later today.

Snatching up the phone again, he punched in Cara's number, then swore hotly at the sound of her recorded voice. He wanted to wring her neck and break that infernal machine into a thousand pieces.

He slammed the phone down again. What was she so mad about, anyway? Of course he'd called her brothers and told them about the danger she was in. Someone had tried to kill her, for God's sake. She needed someone to watch out for her. How could he leave if he didn't know she was taken care of?

A muscle twitched in his jaw. He wasn't trying to ease

his conscience, dammit. He had no reason to feel guilty. He'd done everything he could to protect her. He still was.

He cared about her. More than he'd ever cared about anyone. If anything happened to her...

The thought was like a fist in his gut, and he sank onto the edge of the bed. His heart pounded like a drum in his chest and echoed in the emptiness there.

She would be fine. How could she not be? She was too full of life, too vibrant. Too beautiful and courageous and—

Good God. He dragged a hand through his hair. Next thing he knew he'd be on his knees singing love songs.

He laughed at the image, then shook his head. In another life, maybe there would have been a way to make it work. But this life was too complicated, too uncertain. He couldn't—wouldn't—ask anyone to share that uncertainty with him.

Still, he had to know that she was all right before he left. He couldn't be thinking about her when he went on this mission. It could jeopardize lives if he didn't have a clear, focused mind.

He was reaching for the phone again when the knock at the door stopped him.

"Killian?" Margaret knocked again.

"Yeah." He scrubbed a hand over his face. "Come on in."

He rose from the bed as his grandmother opened the door. She looked a little tired this morning, he thought, and the black pantsuit she wore had a somber tone.

"You didn't come down for breakfast." She stood straight, both hands on her cane and swept her gaze approvingly over the new blue cotton button-up shirt and denim jeans he had on. She'd bought them for him yesterday, despite his insistence he could manage another day in the clothes he had on.

"I'm sorry. I had some phone calls to make."

Margaret gave him an understanding nod. "She's a stubborn one, that girl. Strange, isn't it, how the trait you admire most in a person, is often the one that drives you crazy?"

That pretty much summed up his feelings about Cara, he thought. He did admire that stubborn determination of hers, but it made him want to break things at the same time.

"We need to talk before you leave, Killian." She walked to the window and looked out into the rose garden below. "You need to know a few things…to be prepared when the time comes…"

Her words were like a hand around his heart, gently squeezing. He'd never felt anything like this before. He didn't want to. "I'm sure that's not necessary," he said awkwardly.

She glanced at him, considering, then returned her gaze to the flowers outside. "Thirty-three years ago, when your father died, part of me died along with him," she said quietly. "There's no greater loss, no deeper grief, than the loss of a child. Then, when your grandfather died five years later, it seemed too much to bear. I had three choices— accept what life had handed me and wallow in my grief, end my life, or believe in something greater than myself and get on with the job of living life to its fullest. The first two choices were unthinkable for me, so I went with the third."

He couldn't imagine this woman choosing any other way. "Is that when you took over my grandfather's company?"

"The initial resistance from the all-male board members was strong. It seemed quite hopeless at first. But if there was anything your grandfather taught me, it was never to back down from a difficult situation. Not in business, and certainly not in matters of the heart.''

She paused, her gaze resting firmly on him. From the beginning, there'd been no subtlety in Margaret's match-making between Cara and him. He knew what she wanted, a full-time grandson who came with a wife and great-grandbabies. But he couldn't give that to her, so it was easier, and kinder, to say nothing.

Birds chattered in the elm tree outside the window, and from a neighboring house came the distant hum of a lawn-mower.

With a sigh she placed both hands on her cane and con-tinued, ''Once they learned I wasn't going to go away, they worked with me, and eventually they even accepted me. Five years ago, when I began to feel the limitations of age, I brought Peter in to help manage the firm. Two years ago, after a minor heart disturbance, I stepped down and let him run things. I went into the office every day, but there was nothing for me to do. Once again, I thought my life was over. And then Cara showed up.''

She could do that, Ian thought. Brighten a room just by walking into it, fill an empty space with just a look or a touch. ''She's crazy about you, too.''

Margaret's smile warmed her dark brown eyes. ''We be-came friends, then business partners, and before long I came to love her as my own child. She was the daughter I never had. Two months ago I decided to add her to my will, splitting everything equally between her and Peter. I knew she'd make a fuss about it, so I never told her.''

He went still at his grandmother's words. She was leav-ing Cara half of her estate? An icy sliver of dread crept up from the base of his spine.

"Margaret," he asked carefully, "does Peter know about this?"

She shook her head. "It's not something we've ever spoken about. It was always understood he'd inherit my estate. But Peter lives a fairly simple life, and he already has a large trust fund his father left him, so even with only half of my estate, he would have more money than he would ever need."

Few people ever had more money than they thought they needed. Even someone who lived a simple life. *He knows,* Ian thought. Somehow, he found out.

It all made sense now. Dammit, it all made sense.

It was Peter.

Ian had never suspected his cousin because Cara had been the target. There'd been no apparent reason Peter would want her dead. But with Cara standing to inherit half of Margaret's estate, there was one hell of a reason.

It had been easy for him. He knew her travel arrangements, where she was, what she was doing. He'd hired someone, professionals, to arrive before her so it would look less suspicious. A simple car accident in the mountains of a small town, or an exploding water heater—who would have questioned her death?

"But, anyway," Margaret said with a wave of her hand, "once Cara found you, everything changed."

Ian jerked his attention back to his grandmother. "What's changed?"

"I've changed my will again."

"Margaret." He didn't want to hurt her feelings, but there was no other way to say it. "I'm sorry, but I don't want your money."

"I seem to be surrounded by stubborn." She shook her head. "But I had the feeling you'd say that, so I made a provision with your trust fund, as well as Cara's and Peter's. If any of you choose not to accept your inheritance, it will be donated to the new foundation I'm starting.''

She was going way too fast for him. "Excuse me?''

"I'm starting a new foundation.'' Her eyes sparkled with pleasure. "For unwed and single mothers. The foundation will give them a place to go, money to help them learn job skills to take care of themselves and to provide child care. No woman should have to abandon a baby she loves because of money.''

Her expression was tender as she reached out to touch his face. "No grandmother should be deprived of a child she loves, either. Half of my estate will now be going to the Killian Shawnessy Foundation. If I can keep just one family together, then every dollar, every penny will be worth it.''

The Killian Shawnessy Foundation?

Staggered by the thought, Ian stared at his grandmother. The gentle touch of her hand on his cheek brought a strange tightening in his chest.

Family. The reality of it hit him. She was his family. She had a connection with him, a bond, that no one else in the world did. The thought humbled him, and stunned him, as well.

But the realization, and the implications, of what she'd just told him came crashing down on him.

"Margaret,'' he said as calmly as he could manage, "does anyone else know about this?''

She shook her head. "No. I was waiting for my lawyers to finalize the paperwork, then I was going to announce the foundation's opening at a surprise celebration fund-raiser.''

There would definitely be surprise, but Ian seriously doubted that Peter would consider the event a celebration.

He moved quickly to the phone and dialed.

"Cara, pick up the phone. This is important, pick it up.''

She wasn't going to answer, dammit. "All then, just listen to me. I'm on my way over right now. Don't answer your door until I get there, and don't let anyone in."

He hung up the phone, but for Margaret's sake, he restrained his temper, as well as his fear, then dialed the cell phone number that Gabe had given him. He answered on the first ring. "Is she still in her apartment?" Ian asked.

"Yes," Gabe answered. "Everything looks fine."

"I'll be right over." He hung up the phone and snatched his car keys from the nightstand.

"Killian, what's wrong?" She brought her hand to her throat. "Who were you just talking to?"

In spite of his need to hurry, he moved to his grandmother's side, then surprised them both by kissing her on the cheek. "When I get back, we have some things to talk about. Things about me you should know."

He started for the door, then turned back to her. "Do you have a cell phone?" he asked.

"You don't have a cell phone?" She frowned at him. "I thought you made them."

"That's partly what we need to talk about, but later. Do you have one?"

"In the kitchen, in the battery charger. Killian, whatever this is all about, promise me you'll be careful, won't you?"

"I promise," he said for the first time in his life, and meant it. When he ran out of the bedroom, he left her to stare after him and wonder.

Showered and dressed, Cara came out of the bathroom and almost felt human again. She wasn't certain she looked human, not with the dark circles under her red eyes. But lack of sleep and reading computer files for the past twenty hours was hardly what could be considered a beauty treatment.

Crying didn't do much to improve one's appearance, either, she thought with a sigh.

Damn Killian Shawnessy. He'd reduced her to one of those blubbering, pathetic females. For that she could never forgive him.

There were six messages from him on her machine. She'd been standing next to the phone, or pacing beside it, with each and every one. Each call she'd been torn between picking up the phone and begging him to stay or yelling at him to just go back to Washington and leave her alone.

Coward that she was, she'd compromised by not answering the phone at all.

Twenty-four hours ago they'd made love in her bed. Just the thought of his hands on her skin, his mouth on hers, made her pulse skip. But it hadn't been enough. When it came to Ian, she'd needed more than the physical, could never have settled for less than his heart, too.

All or nothing. For her, that was the only way it could have been.

But that was then and this was now. And right now she needed a good, strong jolt of caffeine. Once she gave her brain a jump start, she'd be fine, she told herself. Just fine.

She was already on her way to the kitchen when the knock at her door stopped her cold. It couldn't be Ian. He would be on his way to the airport now. Unless...

Her legs were trembling as she moved to the door and looked through the peephole.

Her heart sank. It was Peter.

She drew in a deep breath and forced a smile as she opened the door. "Morning," she said, mustering up an enthusiasm she didn't feel at all.

"Good morning." The peck he gave her on the cheek was as crisp as his Armani suit and tie. "You're looking a little peaked this morning. Something wrong?"

"Long night," she said truthfully. "Come on in. I was just about to make some coffee." She shut the door behind him and headed for the kitchen. "Want some?"

"Love it." He touched the rim of his glasses and looked around her living room at the files spread over her couch and coffee table. "What's this?"

She debated, then decided maybe she could use an ear this morning. Besides, if she were talking, she wouldn't have to think about Ian. While she measured coffee and filled the decanter with water, she gave Peter a brief account of what had happened in Wolf River, carefully leaving out the details of her relationship with Ian.

Eyes narrowed behind his glasses, Peter listened, his lips pressed tightly together. "And you have no idea who's trying to kill you," he said when she'd finished.

"Not yet." The smell of brewing coffee already perked up her dimmed senses. "The most likely suspects are in jail, and my number one pick, Margaret's accountant who embezzled the largest amount of all, committed suicide. I'll have to dig deeper and see if any of them have families with revenge on their mind. You want cream with your coffee?"

He shook his head wearily, then sat at the kitchen table, closing his eyes as if in pain.

"Peter, what's wrong?" Cara set the coffee mugs on the table and sat beside him, touched his shoulder with her hand. "Are you sick?"

His laugh was dry. "You know why I came over here this morning?" He looked at her, reached for her hand. "To ask you to marry me."

Marry him? She blinked, stunned by his announcement. "Peter, I…I don't know what to say. I couldn't—"

"I know. Of course, I know. Even after I saw the way you looked at Ian, I still hoped." With a sigh, he let go of her hand. "But a desperate man thinks and does foolish things, Cara. It just would have made everything so much easier. We could have had it all, together."

The look in his eyes, so distant, so empty, made her skin crawl. "What are you talking about, we could have had it all?" she asked. "Why are you desperate?"

"I had a trust fund, you know. A large one. But I wasn't as lucky with money as Margaret. Everything I invested in went sour, and even the gambling turned on me."

"Gambling?" she repeated. "You?"

He took off his glasses and rubbed at his eyes. "Four years ago it started off as a hobby, a little excitement in my mundane, boring existence. I was actually quite good at it. Until a couple of years ago. I got in with the wrong people, the wrong game. Most of my trust fund was gone and they weren't the sort of people to take an IOU. I needed money, a lot of it."

Peter. My God, she thought, dazed by the realization. "You," she gasped. "You embezzled the money."

He nodded, replaced his glasses and sighed. "I was certain I'd be able to replace it before anyone found out. But then the accountant approached me, told me he'd found out and was going to tell Margaret. I couldn't risk that, don't you see?"

He took her hand again, this time squeezed her fingers painfully in his. "I couldn't."

"He didn't commit suicide," she whispered. "You killed him."

"I'm not a killer," he insisted. "But for a price, anything can be bought." He looked at her soulfully. "This is all Margaret's fault, you know. If she hadn't changed her will to include you, I wouldn't have been forced to such extreme measures."

Changed her will? He's crazy, Cara thought wildly.

"You're wrong, Peter. Margaret wouldn't leave me anything. She knows I don't want anything."

"That's what you say now." Peter's face hardened, his eyes turned cold. "You'd have taken it. Money does that to people, makes them want more and more, and it's never enough. And now that you found Ian, she'd have changed the will again and given him the rest. I wouldn't get a nickel."

"Peter, listen to me," she said gently, ignoring the pain in her hand from his crushing grip. "We need to go to the police. We'll get you help. Whatever you need."

He released her suddenly, shook his head. "It's too late now, too complicated. If you had looked deeper during your investigation, you would have eventually found out that I was the one who embezzled Margaret's money. I'm afraid there's going to have to be another suicide, a rejected lover. That's what you are, aren't you? And Margaret will be so distraught, she'll accidentally take an overdose of heart medication."

He sighed heavily and rose from his chair. "If it's any consolation, I won't have to bother with Ian. Margaret won't have time to change her will again."

"It was you," she whispered. "My car, the attempted break-in, the cabin exploding. You did all that."

"No." He walked to the door and opened it. "Not me."

A man and woman stepped into the room. They looked familiar...

The honeymoon couple from Wolf River? She searched her mind...Bob and Pamela Waters. But what were they doing here?

They moved into the room and closed the door behind them. Cara looked from the couple back to Peter. "I don't understand."

"You will," the woman said and lifted a gun. "Very soon."

They all turned at the sound of the ringing phone.

"Don't answer it," Peter snapped.

After three rings, the machine came on…

"Cara, pick up this phone," Ian's voice said. "This is important, pick it up…"

"She's still in there," Gabe told Ian. "Lucian's watching the back, but no one's come in or out all morning, except for the landlady and a tenant on the first floor. You want me to come up with you?"

"Better stay down here. It might get ugly, especially after I tell her a few things about myself." Ian saw Gabe's eyebrows raise, but this wasn't the time to elaborate. "Don't be surprised if she throws me out of her living room window."

"Wouldn't surprise me at all."

The two men shook hands, took measure of each other. "But if you hurt my sister," Gabe said, "I'm afraid I'll have to kill you."

Ian smiled. "I'll do my damnedest not to call your hand on that one."

Dodging a white delivery van as he crossed the street, Ian slipped inside the building, then moved cautiously up the stairwell. The only sound was a radio playing Led Zeppelin from a downstairs apartment and the muffled voice of someone singing along. The aroma of Italian food wafted from the bottom floor, reminding him he'd had nothing more than coffee today.

There was no answer when he knocked on her door. He called her name. Still no answer.

Retrieving Cara's hideaway key that he'd watched Gabe slip back into its cubbyhole yesterday morning, he opened the door. When he stepped inside, he froze at the press of hard steel against his temple.

"Come in, Mr. Shawnessy." The man holding the gun kicked the door shut. "We've been waiting for you."

The man patted him down for a weapon. Ian could easily take the guy, but at the sight of Cara sitting at the kitchen table, his blood went cold.

Her arms were tied behind her; a woman with red hair stood over her, a gun in her hand that she held pressed to Cara's head. Her face was pale, but he saw something in her eyes that gave him hope: anger. Red-hot anger. He wasn't certain who it was directed at, probably everyone, but the fact that it was there gave him a balance he might not have had otherwise.

That's my girl, he thought. Just stay mad and we'll fight them together.

"Well, if it isn't the honeymooners," Ian quipped when the man shoved him into the room. "We never had the privilege of an introduction, did we, kids?"

"You should have left when you were supposed to, cousin." Uncrossing his legs, Peter rose from the living room sofa. "It would have been so much easier."

"It was him all along." Cara glared at Peter. "He hired these two morons to kill me in Wolf River."

Ian winced as the redhead backhanded Cara across the cheek, whipping her head to the side. And with a gun stuck in his back, Ian didn't dare move. Cara's eyes spit green nails as she stared at the other woman.

"You can't get away with this." Ian turned his attention back to Peter. "There are two men watching the front and rear."

Peter's brows lifted in surprise, then he shrugged. "All the better. We came in through the service entrance on the side. With both of you dead, there'll be nothing to connect me to any wrongdoings. In fact, I'm at my office right now, in a meeting. I'll slip back in through my private entrance in the rear, and no one will be the wiser.''

"Margaret changed her will, Peter.''

Peter's head jerked up. "What are you talking about?''

"The will she had drawn up dividing everything between you and Cara? She changed it already. Her new will leaves half of her estate to a foundation she's starting for single mothers.''

"That's a lie.'' Peter's face drained of color. "She wouldn't.''

Desperately wanting to draw the redhead away from Cara, Ian inched toward the table. "Margaret knows the money doesn't mean anything to Cara, and she thinks you have your own inheritance from your father. She doesn't know how seriously in debt you are, or that you've been embezzling from her company.''

One of Ian's phone calls from the cell phone had confirmed his first accusation, but he was guessing on the embezzling part. Based on the angry flush on Peter's face, he'd guessed right.

Peter dragged a shaky hand through his hair, then glanced up at Bob. "I need a few minutes to make some phone calls before you take care of them. Tie him up and wait until I'm finished.''

"The police are on their way now,'' Ian lied. "I called them on the way over here. You can't get away.''

"That's where you're wrong.'' Peter pulled a cell phone out of his pocket, dialed, then nodded to the man standing behind Ian. "Dead wrong, as a matter of fact.''

Ian felt the drop of the gun butt on the back of his neck, heard Cara's cry as he sank to his knees. His head swam with white stars as Bob jerked him back up, then tossed him in the chair beside Cara and tied his hands. With a smile on her face, the redhead ran the gun over Cara's jaw, silently inviting Ian to make a move.

"Hey, Shawnessy." Cara looked directly into his eyes. "That record I told you about, I think I broke it."

Record? What record? He pushed through the fog in his brain, slowly brought his head up as he realized what she was talking about.

The ropes.

He couldn't see behind her back, but he knew she'd broken loose of the ropes holding her. He also knew she was planning something he didn't like.

Peter's face was a tight mask of rage as he turned back to them and snapped his cell phone shut. "My sources tell me that my dear cousin here is telling the truth."

Ian smiled. "Ain't life a bitch?"

"This changes a few things." Peter's eyes narrowed as he looked at Ian and Cara. "But not everything. The headline story tomorrow will still be about a lovers' quarrel gone sour. You'll both have your five minutes of fame, and after Margaret's untimely demise, well, I'll still get half of a great deal of money."

"Peter," Cara appealed. "Just walk away now and no one's been hurt. We'll all just forget about this."

He shook his head sadly, moved next to her and cupped her chin in his hand. "You are my biggest regret, Cara. I truly am sorry."

Her eyes leveled with his. "Not as sorry as you're going to be," she said evenly, then slid her gaze to Ian.

Dammit! Ian recognized that look, that bull-dogged determination. He watched her suck in a breath as Peter turned away, saw her body tense. *No,* he told her with his eyes, but she only nodded.

His hands were bound tight enough to cut off circulation

at his wrists, but Bob was still working at his ankles. Ian braced himself.

Cara shot out of the chair like a cannonball, fists flying as she whirled on the redhead at the same time Ian slammed his head downward and rammed Bob's nose.

That's when all hell broke loose.

The redhead's gun exploded; the bullet blasted the ceiling, raining plaster all over them. Peter raised an arm to cover his head while he ran for the front door, but at the moment, Ian had other, more immediate problems than Peter's escape. Bob was gushing blood from his nose and mad as hell as he reared up from the floor.

Ian kicked out with his half-tied feet, made direct contact with the man's groin. Doubling over, Bob toppled into the dining room table, sucking in air. Ian kicked out a second time, catching the man in the nose again. Howling with pain, he crashed into the wall, knocking down pictures and a shelf with china. Plates and teacups smashed onto his head; his eyes rolled backward, then his head dropped limply onto his chest.

Whirling, ready to help Cara, Ian couldn't help but smile when he saw her kneeling on the facedown, laid-out redhead.

"You all right, Blondie?" he asked.

"Just fine, Flash." Breathing hard, she reached for the rope she'd escaped from, then twisted the moaning redhead's arms behind her back. "You?"

Ian glanced at the unconscious man lying on the floor and nodded. "Peter got away."

The door burst open with a splintering roar. Both Ian and Cara whirled, ready to fight. Gabe stormed into the room, his body crouched and ready for battle. He slowly relaxed as his gaze darted around the shattered dining room.

"You guys all right?" Gabe moved behind Ian and untied the ropes holding his hands.

At the sound of crunching wood, they all tensed and turned again.

Lucian stepped through the doorway, shoving a battered Peter in front of him. "Look who I found coming out the side," he said, then took in the disarmed man and woman on the floor. "Gosh, looks like I missed all the fun."

Ian knelt beside Cara, touched a nasty welt rising on her forehead. "You could have been killed," he said around the lump in his throat.

"What are you doing here, Ian?" Her eyes slid over his face. "You're supposed to be gone."

He held her steady gaze. "I came back."

"Did you?"

"Yeah." He smiled slowly. "I did."

Thirteen

Police sirens set every dog howling within a two-block radius. Guns drawn, uniformed officers crowded the stairwell, then swarmed into the apartment. Good guys were sorted from bad guys, statements taken, with only a few moments of excitement when Bob woke up and decided he didn't want to be handcuffed. Fortunately the police convinced him otherwise.

When the adrenaline pumping through Cara's body turned her numb, she let Ian lead her away from the garbled static of police radios, away from the rubble that had once been her dining room, and into the quiet of the bedroom.

He made her sit on the edge of the bed. When she started to protest, he pointed a finger under her nose.

"Stay here," he ordered. "I'll be back."

"That's what Arnold Schwarzeneggar says just before something explodes." Her sarcasm earned her a smile, but he said nothing, just turned on his heels and left the room.

When he came back no more than two minutes later, first aid kit and wet washcloth in hand, she was humiliated that he found her shivering.

"Oh, baby," he murmured, wrapped the bedspread around her, then sat on the bed and gathered her in his arms.

"I think there's a window open somewhere." The warmth of his strong arms felt wonderful, and she burrowed herself into his chest.

"You don't have to be embarrassed, Sinclair." He rocked her, brushed his lips against her temple. "It's normal to go into shock after someone points a gun at your head."

"I'm not in shock," she insisted, was furious when her teeth started chattering. "And why do you know so much about guns and what's normal, anyway?"

"I know."

She went still at the sober tone of his words, then pushed away and looked up at him. "How do you know?"

He sighed heavily. "I'm not exactly who you think I am, Cara."

Her hands were trembling now, and she pulled the bedspread tightly around her. "Go on."

"I work for a high-level government agency," he said evenly. "My assignments are normally out of the country, usually dangerous and always covert."

Either she'd been hit on the head too hard or he had. "You mean top-secret?"

"Yes."

He was teasing her, she decided. Trying to lighten a serious situation. "So now that you've told me," she said, forcing a smile, "you have to kill me, right?"

He didn't smile back.

She blinked, looked for the lie in his eyes, but found none. "You're serious, aren't you?"

"I'm afraid so."

It took her a minute to let his words, then the reality sink in. He was a government agent. Undercover.

Her mind was spinning and she closed her eyes, drew in a slow breath to steady herself. It would explain so much. The gun he carried, his reaction to her when he'd caught her spying on him by the lake, the way he'd handled Bob the hit man.

It had been there all along, right under her nose. She'd been so focused on her goal, she'd never seen the obvious.

But she knew she'd missed it for another reason, too, and the truth of it stung. She'd fallen for him, hard, and her emotions had blinded her.

She felt like a fool.

"Cairo," she whispered, and the shiver she felt now had nothing to do with guns or bad guys. "You aren't going to Cairo for your company. That was a lie, too, wasn't it? You're going on an assignment."

"Not anymore." He took her by the arms, turned her to face him. "I missed my briefing. It's going to get a little complicated, but Jordan is going to have to send someone else."

"Jordan?" It took a moment, but she remembered the woman who'd called him at the cabin was named Jordan. "Your business associate?"

"My boss." Brushing her hair away from her face, he reached for the wet washcloth and pressed it to the fiery welt on her cheek. "At least, she was my boss."

"Was?"

"I'm going to choose another assignment. One she has no jurisdiction over."

Her heart sank. Three times already she'd had to prepare

herself for his leaving: at the cabin; their first night in Philadelphia; then last night again. How could she survive a fourth?

She should be furious at him. She'd certainly earned the right to give him a big piece of her mind. He'd lied to her, deceived her. She should demand he leave right now, tell him she couldn't stand to even look at him.

But she loved him. *She'd* be the liar if she pretended anything else. After what they'd gone through together, she only loved him more. Nothing else mattered. Not that he'd lied, or who he was. Or what he was. To her, he was simply Killian Shawnessy. He was everything.

"Will you come back?" she asked, hating the pathetic sound of her voice.

"It's a long assignment," he said solemnly. "Very long."

"How long?" She didn't care if it was a hundred years. If he wanted her, she'd wait.

"The rest of my life."

Confused, she frowned at him. "The rest of your life?"

He nodded. "The thing is, I need a partner. But it's a dangerous and very risky assignment. I wouldn't ask just anyone. It takes a very special woman."

She had to remind herself to breathe. "What's the assignment?"

He cupped her chin in his hand and tipped her face up to his. "Marriage." There was a slight tremble in his voice. "To me."

Her heart, which had felt like lead only a moment before, skipped lightly into her throat. He wanted to *marry* her?

If he was teasing, she couldn't stand it. She swallowed, forced a light tone to ward off the threatening tears.

"Gosh, I don't know, Shawnessey. That *is* dangerous. Does this position come with fringe benefits?"

"A house, probably. Maybe a dog." He brushed his thumb over her lip. "But the hours will be long, well into the night, every night."

She raised her brows. "*Every* night? That's an ambitious assignment, Flash."

"Okay, most nights." He smiled, then sucked in a breath. "And kids, Blondie. God help me, I want kids. You up for the job or not?"

She hesitated, still uncertain if she were asleep and this was a cruel dream. But the warm touch of his hand on her skin was real, the feel of his body pressed against hers solid.

He wanted to marry her. Have *children.*

A giddiness overtook her, one of those silly, female outbursts that she'd always abhorred. She caught them both off guard when she flew at him, sent them both tumbling to the floor wrapped in the bedspread and each other. Her mouth found his, and she kissed him soundly, deeply, luxuriating in the feel and taste of him.

"Say it." She rolled on top of him, pinned him underneath her. "Say it, Flash."

He grinned up at her. "I love you, Sinclair. Will you marry me?"

"Yes," she breathed. "Yes, yes, *yes.* And I love you, too."

He kissed her again, deeply, tenderly, and she felt the heavy thud of his heart under hers.

"I've lived alone all my life," he said carefully. "I thought that was enough, all I'd ever need. And then you showed up, all fire and sass, and you had me hooked from that first day."

"The first day, huh?" She raised a brow and smiled. "So you *are* into tying a woman up, are you?"

He rolled his eyes at her nonsense. "When you walked

out of that bathroom so damn smug, laughing at me with those incredible eyes of yours, I was a goner, Sinclair.''

His admission took her breath away, and also brought the tears she'd been struggling against. "I think I loved you from the first minute I laid eyes on you, Shawnessy. Standing on that cabin porch, looking like the lone hunter. Daring anyone to invade his territory. You were magnificent.''

She'd never seen him blush before, didn't know he could, but there was pleasure in his eyes, as well.

"I thought I could walk away," he murmured. "Thought that I'd be able to let you go. I was a fool.''

Grinning, she brushed her lips with his. "Don't forget pigheaded and stubborn.''

He grinned back at her. "I may not be easy to live with.''

She laughed at that. "And you think I will?''

He laughed, too. "We're quite a team, Blondie.''

"You got that right, Flash.''

He kissed her as he never had before—with love and a promise for tomorrow. There were details, so many details, she thought dimly as she kissed him back. But what did they matter?

After all, details were her specialty.

*   *   *   *   *

Coming this September 1999
from SILHOUETTE BOOKS
and bestselling author
RACHEL LEE

CONARD COUNTY:
Boots & Badges

Alicia Dreyfus—a desperate woman on the run—is about to discover that she *can* come home again...to Conard County. Along the way she meets the man of her dreams—and brings together three other couples, whose love blossoms beneath the bold Wyoming sky.

Enjoy four complete, **brand-new** stories in one extraordinary volume.

Available at your favorite retail outlet.

PSCCBB

The O'Connors

A collection of two complete novels
by award-winning author

Karen Young

In the O'CONNORS Karen Young works her
magic with riveting tales of a brother and
sister, each caught in controversy, danger
and love beyond their control.

Available September 1999 at your favorite retail outlet.

HARLEQUIN®
Makes any time special ™

Look us up on-line at: http://www.romance.net

PSBR2999

THE FORTUNES OF TEXAS

*Membership in this family has its privileges
…and its price.
But what a fortune can't buy,
a true-bred Texas love is sure to bring!*

Coming in October 1999…

The Baby Pursuit

by

LAURIE PAIGE

When the newest Fortune heir was kidnapped, the
prominent family turned to Devin Kincaid to find the
missing baby. The dedicated FBI agent never expected
his investigation might lead him to the altar with
society princess Vanessa Fortune.…

THE FORTUNES OF TEXAS continues with
Expecting… In Texas by **Marie Ferrarella**,
available in November 1999 from
Silhouette Books.

Available at your favorite retail outlet.

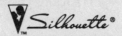

Silhouette®